ENCHANTED SPELLS

(Witches of Bayport)

BOOK THREE

Kristen Middleton

CHAPTER ONE

Kala

"Kala, have you seen that book we put aside for Mrs. Martin?" called out Beatrice from the front of the store. She was the owner of Bea's Books, where I'd been working as a clerk for the past three months. It was a small shop, two blocks away from *Secrets*, where my twin sister Kendra was now working part-time.

"It's under the counter," I said loudly.

"I don't see it anywhere," she replied, frustrated.

Sighing, I shut the spell book I'd been leafing through, slid it back into the shelf, and walked around the aisle. Sure, I wasn't exactly working, but there really wasn't too much to do besides dusting and reading.

"Never mind. I found it," she said, pulling it out from where I'd left it. "Wouldn't you know – it was right in front of my face."

"Of course it was," I mumbled as she stood up straight and set the book down on the counter.

She raised a brow. "What was that, dear?"

"I said that I'm glad that you found it."

She laughed dryly. "No, that's not what you said. I might be blind but I'm not deaf. Are we in a funk today?"

I stared back at the tall, thin woman with the frizzy, red hair and purple horn-rimmed glasses. As much as she'd been getting on my nerves lately, I actually really like Bea. Not only had she given me my first job, but she'd been helping me learn a few harmless spells with my wand named Penelope.

I sighed and ran a hand through my hair. "Sorry. I'm just a little tired, I guess."

She walked around the counter, studying my face intently. "Tired, huh? You haven't been staying up all night reading the spell book you took from the store a couple of days ago, have you?"

I gave her a wide-eyed stare. "Spell book? What do you mean?"

Bea gave me a disapproving look. "You know *exactly* what I mean. Kala, I don't care if you borrow any of the books in this store, as long as you are honest about doing it."

"I'm sorry," I said, my face turning red. I wasn't even sure why I'd kept it from her. Now I felt foolish. "And, you're absolutely right. I should have told you about the book."

"Yes, you should have. Especially *that* kind of book. It's dangerous."

I wondered how she'd known which one I'd taken. It was a very old book about Black magic. It had caught my eye the other day, when I'd been locking up the store. "Don't worry. I was very careful with it," I replied. "And... I didn't read anything out loud." I'd heard that even thinking the words to some of the dark spells could invoke something terrible.

Bea relaxed. "Well, thank goodness for that. I'd hate to have anything bad happen, especially to you, young lady. I'd have to try and find someone to fill your position, and I loathe doing interviews."

I smiled, remembering our brief one. She'd asked me my age, my knowledge on magic, and if I was punctual. Right afterward, she'd offered me a job on the spot. "Yeah, I'd hate to inconvenience you like that."

She chortled loudly. "You know I'm only joking. I have to admit – you *were* an easy hire. You had wonderful references, though."

And of course, you have Penelope.

"What did you say?" I asked, surprised.

She gave me a blank look. "You had wonderful references?"

"No. What were you saying about Penelope?"

"I didn't say anything," said Bea, looking at me curiously. "What did you think I said about your wand?"

I was about to tell her exactly what I thought I'd heard her say, when something made me hesitate.

"Kala?" asked Bea, coming closer. "What is it?"

I laughed it off. "Nothing. I'm tired. You were right. I did stay up late looking through that old book and now my head is cloudy. You wouldn't mind if I left early tonight, would you?" It was just after eight p.m. and the shop closed at nine.

She waved her hand toward the empty aisles. "Obviously I can handle this all on my own. Just... do us both a favor and get yourself a good night's sleep."

"I will."

"Good. And by the way, I am still going to need you to open the store tomorrow. I have a breakfast engagement."

"I remember. Don't worry. I'll be here. I promise."

"Where is that book, by the way?"

"The one that I took home?"

"Yes."

"I brought it back this morning. It's up there," I said, nodding toward the second level, where there were two enchanted bookcases. One held White magic books, the other, Black. Only true wizards and witches were able to see what the shelves actually held, however. To anyone else, they appeared empty.

"Good. From now on, if you want to look through any of those spell books, ask me. We'll do it together."

"I will."

She patted me on the shoulder and then walked back toward the register. "Now, off with you."

"Are you sure? I can stick around and help you stock the new books that came in today before I leave."

"No. Don't worry about it. I have to price them, which I plan on doing tomorrow."

"Okay."

"One more thing – say hello to Clarice for me, will you?" said Bea, removing her eyeglasses. She sprayed them with something and began cleaning them.

"If I see her. She's been in Oregon for some knitting convention," I replied heading toward the backroom to gather my purse and coat.

"That's right."

When I returned a few moments later, Bea asked, "Do you need a ride home or are you going to call Bailey for one?"

"I'm going to walk," I replied, buttoning my black wool jacket. I hadn't spoken to him in a few days. Not after he'd given me the third degree about Penelope again. He'd been nagging me about disposing of it, worried that it would somehow corrupt me. Since then, I'd been avoiding his calls and texts. Although I still liked Bailey a lot, I wasn't about to let a wand, or him, for that matter, control me.

"It's very chilly outside. Are you sure?"

I bit back a smile. It could be eighty degrees and Bea would need a sweater. "I'll be fine. This jacket is quite warm. Besides, it's snowing out there and is a lovely night for a walk." I nodded toward the window at the light dusting of snow.

Bea walked over to the window and looked up at the sky. "It sure is. Maybe even a nice night to fly a broom. Did you get one yet?"

"No."

She nodded toward the back of the store. "I've got a couple spares in back. Feel free to choose one for yourself."

I wanted a broom, but not any old one. Penelope said I needed to find one that was worthy enough for the both of us. I thought back to the conversation we'd had the other night.

"You're special, as am I. Now that we're a team, it's imperative that you begin to realize the significance of our union."

"That's the problem. I still don't completely understand why I'm able to hold you," I replied warily. *Even though I'd been thrilled that such a powerful wand had allowed me to bond with her, the fact that she was used mainly for dark magic was a little unnerving.*

"I feel your fear, but it is unwarranted. Just remember, you are in control of the spells cast through me. Yes, I've been created for the dark arts, but I can also be used for good, if my witch demands it."

"You can?" I asked, a wave of relief flooding through me.

"Of course. That's why I'm much more powerful than Chloe, or any other wand, for that matter," she replied arrogantly. *"As you will be much more powerful than Kendra."*

Her words had given me mixed feelings. I loved my sister and didn't want to have anything on her. But I had to admit, the thought of having a more powerful wand was a little exhilarating.

"I don't want to be more powerful than my sister," I replied, the words sounding weak even to myself.

"Maybe not now, but that will change," she'd said, a smile in her voice.

I frowned. "What do you mean?"

"You ask too many questions. Some things you must learn on your own."

"But, how can I? I wasn't raised as a witch and right now, everyone wants me to give you up. I'm pretty much on my own here."

She let out a frustrated sigh. "Fine. Do you really want my advice?"

"Sure. I guess."

"Of course you do. You're like a lost lamb right now. Vulnerable and impressionable."

I tried to deny it. "I'm neither. I'm just unsure of where to begin."

"You begin by realizing that you aren't just any witch. You're a descendant of one of the most powerful witches to ever to walk the face of the earth."

"So I've been told," I mumbled under my breath. I knew she was talking about Isadora, but Kendra and I were also Vivian's daughters and that woman was deplorable.

"You should be proud."

"I am."

"Good, because you are exceptional and should always surround yourself with exceptional items. That includes enchanted objects. Take for instance your broom."

"I don't have one."

"Exactly, and when you do select one to use, it has to be worthy."

"Worthy?" There was that word again.

"Of course. A witch's broom becomes a part of her. You must make sure it's fast and strong. Not like some of the hand-me-downs Rebecca is selling in her shop."

"Where am I supposed to find one like that?" I knew I couldn't just walk into Home Depot and browse the broom department.

"Don't worry, child. Your broom will find you."

"When?" I asked, doubtful.

"I'm not a psychic. You'll have to find that out for yourself," she replied in an exasperated voice.

And that had been the end of that conversation. She'd offered me nothing more.

"Kala? Did you want one of my brooms?" repeated Bea.

"No. Thank you, Bea. I prefer to walk, especially since it's still snowing."

"Fine then. Be careful. It might be slippery out there."

I smiled at her concern. "I will, thank you. I'll see you tomorrow? After your breakfast meeting?"

"Yes." She glanced outside and into the sky again. "Call me if you run into any trouble."

"You worry too much," I said, amused.

"Maybe. Maybe not," she answered.

And you have no idea how many people want your wand, do you?

I blinked.

She hadn't spoken, but I'd heard the words, clear as day. As confused as I was, I decided not to say anything. She might think I was crazy, and who knows? Maybe I really was just hearing things.

"Goodnight, Bea."

"Goodnight, Kala," she said, following me to the door. "By the way, how's your mother doing? Is she still sick with that dreadful cold?"

"Yes, but she's doing better."

"Good. Tell her that I said 'Hi'."

"I will. See you."

"Indeed." Bea turned off the 'Open' sign and gave me one last smile as I left the shop.

As I stepped outside and onto the sidewalk, I couldn't help but smile at all of the holiday decorations and lights from the other shops. Unfortunately, our bookstore was the least festive place on the block. I'd asked Bea about it, and she'd claimed that she didn't want to offend any of the witches or warlocks who shopped with us. Apparently some of them balked at anything to do with religion or holidays.

Licking a snowflake that had landed on my lip, I began walking toward Secrets to see if Kendra was still there. They also closed at nine, and chances were that Tyler would be bringing her home, but if not, I wanted to talk to her about possibly hearing Bea's thoughts.

"Kala!"

Recognizing the voice, I looked back over my shoulder and noticed Bailey jogging toward me.

"Hi," I said, forcing a smile to my face as he stopped in front of me. His blonde hair was pulled back into a short ponytail and his cheeks and ears were pink from the chill. "I didn't expect to see you here."

"I know. I wanted to surprise you." Bailey pulled me into his arms and hugged me tightly. "I've missed you so much."

I relaxed, enjoying the smell of his brown leather jacket and something else that was even more pleasing. "You smell like Snickerdoodles."

He laughed and pulled away slightly. "I was in the bakery up the street. They were making Christmas cookies and gave me a couple of free samples."

I stared up into his face and my stomach did a flip-flop. The guy was so gorgeous and here he was, holding little old me in his arms. Although we'd shared a couple of kisses, I still wasn't used to someone like Bailey. Not only was he a shape-shifter, he looked like he belonged on a poster hanging from my wall.

"Were they good?" I asked.

He let me go and then held up a small, white bag. "Heck yeah. They were delicious. Don't worry. I picked a couple up for you. It's actually why I stopped in there in the first place."

It's a bribe.

That voice in my head again? Where was it coming from?

He's going to try and talk you out of keeping the wand again.

Frowning, I crossed my arms under my chest. "So, what is this?" I nodded toward the bag. "A bribe? Or some kind of peace offering?"

He stared at me in confusion. "A bribe? What do you mean?"

"Come on, Bailey. You still want me to get rid of my wand. I know you do."

"Well, yeah. Of course."

"I knew it," I said, frustrated.

He sighed. "Kala, I know you're sick of hearing it, but that wand really is dangerous."

"Not to me."

His brows drew together. "*Especially* to you."

*Maybe he doesn't even care about you...
Maybe... he just wants the wand for himself,*
whispered the voice in my head.

I couldn't believe that. If that was the case, he'd just take it from me.

He can't just take it and it would never bond with him.

"Kala, what's going through your head right now?" asked Bailey, staring into my eyes. "Talk to me."

"Fine," I said sharply. "Let's talk."

He stood there patiently, a puzzled look on his face. As if my anger was a surprise.

"Tell me – did you really come all the way over here just to lecture me again? Because if you did, you may as well take your cookies and shove them–"

"Kala!" scolded a voice behind me. "Where in the world are your manners?"

CHAPTER TWO

Kala

Stiffening up, I turned around. "Mom. What are you doing here? I thought you were at home, sick?"

The look on Adrianne's face made me take a step back. She looked like she was about to grab me by the ear and drag me down the street.

"I've been trying to call you but you haven't been answering your phone. Now, I think you owe Bailey an apology," she said sternly.

My cheeks burned as I turned back to him. "I'm sorry."

"It's okay," he said, searching my eyes. "You realize that I'm just worried about you."

I looked down. "You don't have to be."

"First of all – her behavior is not 'okay'," said Adrianne, pulling a tissue out of her coat. She wiped her nose and shoved it back into her pocket. "I taught you better than that. And in all honesty, he's right. The wand is dangerous and I'm beginning to think that you should get rid of it, too."

"That's not fair," I said, feeling panicky. "I haven't done anything wrong. Nor has Penelope."

"You're obviously not acting like yourself," said Adrianne, now the one looking worried. "And... you're obsessed with that wand."

"I am not *obsessed*," I argued. "In fact, everyone else seems to be the ones who are obsessed with it. I hardly ever even take Penelope out."

"Good, because it's dangerous. Listen to me, Kala, you don't need that wand. There are plenty of others that would serve you well," she said.

"But none as special as Penelope. Besides, she serves me," I said firmly. "I'm the one in control. Not her."

Her eyes narrowed with suspicion. "Control? It's funny that you used that particular phrase. Has Penelope tried to make you do things you didn't want to do?"

I almost laughed. It sounded as if she was talking about something entirely different. "No. The only one trying to make me do things I don't want to, so far, is Bailey."

Her head whipped back to him.

He gave her a crooked smile. "Don't look at me. I haven't put any kind of pressure on her other than getting rid of that wand," Bailey said, his eyes twinkling.

Adrianne relaxed and turned back to me. "Kala, he's just worried about you. So am I."

"I'm not a child anymore," I said, raising my chin. "I'm eighteen and more than capable of handling the wand. You both need to trust me on this."

"I do trust you. I just don't trust the kind of magic that Penelope can invoke," she said, crossing her arms under her chest. "You saw what it did to me."

"As long as nobody else tries touching the wand, there shouldn't be any problems," I said. "And... I'm not giving it up. So give it up."

Bailey muttered something under his breath.

She let out an exasperated groan. "You're so darn stubborn. And about a wand, nonetheless. Just like–" Adrianne stopped.

I raised my eyebrows. "Like Vivian?"

"Yes. But that's the only thing you have in common," she replied, her eyes softening.

"Exactly, and that's why you need to trust me with the wand," I said.

She stared pensively into the darkness and nodded. "Well, if you're not going to give the wand up, then you'll just need to be educated on how to use it properly."

"Bea is teaching me," I answered.

"You need more than Beatrice," she replied with a frown. "For one thing, she never owned a bonding wand, much less one as powerful as Penelope. And two, I don't know the woman enough to trust her."

"Then what do you suggest?" I asked.

"I have some ideas," she replied.

It was then that I noticed my sister and Tyler heading toward us, both of them looking tense.

Bailey noticed them, too. "I should go. Here," he said, holding out the bag of cookies toward me. "And, these *weren't* a 'bribe' or a 'peace offering'. I was just thinking of you."

"That's very nice of you, Bailey," said Adrianne, looking down at the bag. "Isn't it, Kala?"

Not looking him in the eye, I took the bag. "Yes. Thank you."

"You're welcome," he replied and then glanced at my mother again. "Glad to see that you're feeling better, Adrianne."

"Thank you, so am I," she replied as the wind blew her bangs over her eyes. She pushed them out of the way and smiled. "So, where are you off to on this blustery night?"

His lip curled up. "Here and there."

"Here and there, huh? Well, don't be a stranger," she replied. "In fact, we'll have to have you over for dinner soon."

"I'd like that," he replied.

She looked over at me. "Kala is an excellent cook."

I gave her a sideways glance. I was far from being a good cook, let alone an excellent one. "We'll let him judge."

She laughed. "You'll get the hang of it. You just need more practice. Which is why I think having Bailey over will give you incentive to work on your culinary skills."

I snorted. "Right. My culinary skills."

"I love to eat so I'd be happy to test out any of your cooking," he said.

"You say that now..." I said, smiling.

"I'm sure whatever you make will be good. Anyway, I'd better go. I will be watching for an invitation in my mailbox," Bailey said before leaning over and kissing me quickly on the lips. "Goodbye," he said, smiling as he pulled away.

"Goodbye," I replied, smiling back.

"He likes you a lot, you know," said Adrianne, as we both watched Bailey walk away.

"I know."

"You still like him, don't you?"

"Yes. I still like him," I admitted. As irritated as I was with Bailey and his paranoia about the wand, his presence always gave me butterflies. "I just wish he'd stop nagging me about Penelope."

"I think he's now pretty much resigned to the fact that you're not giving it up. Both of us are."

I grinned. "Good."

"Hi," said Kendra, stopping next to us. She nodded toward Bailey's retreating back. "Where's he off to?"

"I guess here and there," I replied.

Her eyebrows shot up.

"In other words, I have no idea." I looked over at Tyler. "Hi, Tyler."

"Hi," he said, smiling behind his dark sunglasses. "Did we interrupt something? You three looked like you were having quite the conversation."

"Yes, we were, but you aren't interrupting anything," said Adrianne. "In fact, I'm glad that I have my two daughters together for once. We need to talk."

"What is it?" asked Kendra.

Adrianne looked at me and then back at her. "It's about school."

"*School?* Is something wrong? My grades are fine," I said quickly.

"It's nothing like that. Let's head back to *Secrets* and talk about it. I want Willow there, too." She pulled out her phone. "I suppose I'd better send her a message."

"Willow? Why?" I asked.

Willow was now living back in the Devil's Playground with her mother, Opal. Fortunately, the psychiatric hospital had released her into Willow's custody two weeks ago, and from what I'd been told, things were going well.

"Because what I have planned involves her," she replied, texting Willow. When she was finished, she put her phone back into her purse and all three of us followed Adrianne back to S*ecrets*.

"Where's Rebecca?" she asked as Tyler unlocked the door.

"Believe it or not, mom is on a date," he said, with a little smile.

"A date? With whom?" asked Adrianne, looking surprised.

"Tony Belucchi. He owns the meat market up the street," said Tyler.

"I know him. He's very nice, isn't he, girls?" said Adrianne.

We both nodded.

"I'm surprised she didn't mention it," said Adrianne.

"It was a spur of the moment decision. He's been asking her for a while now, and she finally agreed," said Tyler.

I thought about the heavyset guy with the dark hair, bright blue eyes, and twisty moustache. I'd only seen him behind the counter at the butcher shop. He seemed nice enough, but wasn't the type of guy I'd have imagined Rebecca dating.

"Is he a witch, too?" I asked.

"No, and he's not aware that she's one," said my sister. "Which is why Rebecca didn't really want to go out with him in the first place. But, he's been so persistent and sweet, that she finally agreed."

"Hope they're having fun," I said. "By the way, isn't the store supposed to be open until nine?"

"It was dead, so we closed early," said Tyler.

Just then, Willow popped into the room with her mother.

"Oh good," said Adrianne, her face lighting up. "You brought Opal."

Willow smiled. "Mom, you remember Adrianne, don't you?"

Opal nodded. "Yes. We're cousins, I think? She helped move me back to the cabin two weeks ago, too."

"Yes. We are cousins." Adrianne walked up to her and gave her a hug. "How've you been?" she asked, releasing her.

"Good," she replied, smiling weakly. "Now that I'm back home, things are going very well. In fact, I haven't felt this good in a long time."

"It's because you're back with your family," said Adrianne.

"Yes," she answered, her eyes getting misty. "Every day I have to pinch myself, to make sure I'm not dreaming." Opal glanced at Willow. "And that she's real."

"Yeah, me too," said Willow, smiling back at her mother warmly.

"So, what did you want to talk about?" asked Opal. "Your text sounded urgent."

"It is." Adrianne let out a ragged sigh. "Look, I'm sorry to drag you out here in the middle of the night, but we have a situation."

"A situation?" I asked, surprised. "I thought this was about school."

"That's part of it," said Adrianne.

"What's wrong?" asked Kendra, frowning.

"Now, I don't want you to panic. I'm sure everything will be fine, since the three of you are here. Safe and sound," said Adrianne.

"You're scaring me. What's going on?" asked Kendra.

"The enchanted globe holding Vivian and Mark has gone missing," she said. "I think it's been stolen."

Kendra and I stared at each other in shock.

"Has she escaped Winter Bliss?" asked Tyler.

"I don't know. I can't imagine she has. Not with the kind of spell that's been placed on the globe, and with your wand, Kala. A spell like that shouldn't be easily broken."

"Where was the globe when you last saw it?" asked Tyler.

"In that safe in our basement," said Adrianne. "And to be honest, I don't know how long the globe has been missing. I haven't checked the safe in weeks. I only looked tonight because I had this strange feeling that something was wrong."

"Good instinct," said Tyler. "Was the safe broken?"

Adrianne shook her head. "No, it was intact. Nothing seemed amiss, so when I opened it, I really wasn't expecting to find it empty."

"Empty? So, the book was missing, too?" I asked, remembering that she'd also stored Isadora's old spell book inside as well.

"Yes," she said with a grave look. "Which tells me it's probably a dark witch."

"Someone who's trying to help Vivian escape?" asked Kendra.

"Yes or someone who wants to make sure she never escapes," said Opal softly.

"I doubt we could be that lucky," replied Adrianne.

CHAPTER THREE

Bella and Beldora stood over the globe, looking down at Vivian and Mark, who were standing in snow. Both were dressed in parkas and snow boots.

"Still nothing?" asked Bella, who was holding the spell book they'd stolen from Adrianne's safe earlier that day.

"Not that I can tell," said Beldora, frowning. "Try another spell."

Bella flipped through the pages and sighed. "Maybe we should just give it a rest. We've been at it for hours; nothing is working."

Vivian, who could hear them, clenched her fists and began yelling.

"Oh my. She's not happy," whispered Beldora. Neither could hear Vivian but it was obvious she'd heard Bella loud and clear.

"I guess not. Look, we're doing the best we can, Vivian," said Bella loudly. "Don't get mad at us. You were the one who got yourself into this situation."

Vivian's face turned as red as her hair. She raised her fist and shook it at them.

"I don't think you should have said that," murmured Beldora, watching the expression on Mark's face as the woman carried on. Even he looked shocked by whatever it was that Vivian was spouting out. "She looks like she wants to turn you into a pile of rubble."

"Whatever. She should only be angry with herself. Not us," scoffed Bella. "We're trying to help and," she waved her hand toward the globe, "instead of being grateful, she's throwing another fit."

The truth was that the two witches were attempting to free Vivian because they needed *her* help. Semora, who was currently leading the coven, had not only banished Bella and Beldora from the group, but had made sure that no other coven would take them in. They were now black-listed and nobody trusted them. Angry and wanting revenge, they'd decided to try and free Vivian from the globe so she could kill Semora and restore their reputations.

"Maybe we should let her cool down," said Beldora, biting the side of her lip. "I'd hate to free her when she's in a mood."

Having heard this, Vivian's demeanor changed abruptly. She smiled and then clasped her hands together, now pleading with them to keep going.

"She must hear every word we're saying," whispered Bella, with a smirk.

"Apparently."

Vivian nudged Mark, and soon, both of them were on their knees, begging to be released.

"You can't blame them for wanting to get out. It must be horrible.... living in that little ball. Just the two of them," replied, Beldora, shuddering. "I'd go crazy myself. We need to try again."

Vivian nodded, still holding her clasped hands up toward them. "Please," she mouthed.

"Fine. We'll try a few more spells, but then I've got to get back home. I have laundry that needs to be done."

Beldora looked at her watch. "And I need to get back to watch the season finale of 'Breaking Howie'. It's going to be on in fifteen minutes."

"You watch that show? I tried but just couldn't get into it," said Bella.

"It starts out slow but after a couple of episodes, it really gets good. I've been waiting all week to watch the season finale."

"Hmm... maybe I should try watching it again?"

"You really should."

"Although, I'm behind in my Downton Abbey episodes. So many choices, so little time."

***

Vivian gritted her teeth together. Listening to the two women babbling about television was making her shake.

"At this rate, we won't get out of here until summer," muttered Mark, rubbing his wool gloves together.

"Those fools," said Vivian, trying to stay calm. "If they do manage to release us, I'm going to send them here, where there is *no* Downton Abbey or... what was that other show?"

"Breaking Howie. It really is a good show. There's sex, violence –"

Vivian's eyes darkened. "Violence? I'll show them violence if they keep wasting time."

Mark paled. "Do you think they can pull it off?"

She frowned. "To be honest, I think they'll need to get their hands on Willow's wand."

"Juniper?"

"Yes. I thought there'd be a spell in Isadora's book that would have worked on the globe, but Penelope's magic is just too powerful. Juniper should be able to reverse the magic, however."

"Do you really think so?"

"Nothing else seems to be working." She sighed. "I should have had them retrieve the wand to begin with."

"Why didn't you?"

"Because I didn't think that those two nincompoops could handle the task. Stealing the spell book is one thing, but fetching Juniper is an entirely new ballgame. I'm sure Willow sleeps with it under her pillow. But now I don't really see another choice. They need to try and steal it."

"Then let's get their attention so we can get the heck out of here," said Mark, picking up a handful of snow. He made a snowball and threw it toward Bella's and Beldora's faces. Sighing, Vivian leaned down and grabbed a handful of snow.

"I hate winter," she mumbled to herself, vowing that when she did get out, she'd take her revenge out on everyone who deserved it and then move to somewhere tropical.

***

"Looks like they're trying to get our attention again," said Bella, staring back into the globe.

"Hopefully she thought of something that will help us," said Beldora, moving closer.

Vivian said something to Mark and pointed toward the ground. He grabbed a can of paint from his pocket and began spraying another message onto the snow, like he had earlier.

"Reverse the spell with Juniper," said Bella, reading the message out loud.

"Would that work?" asked Beldora, turning toward Bella.

The other witch nodded slowly and smiled. "It reversed the other spells. Why not?"

"Very true. Why didn't we just go and find that wand to begin with?" sighed Beldora.

"I don't know. Maybe she thought the spell book would be enough," said Bella, looking down at the globe. "Apparently it's not."

Nodding in agreement, Vivian gave her two thumbs up.

"Willow still has that wand and you know she's not going to give it up. She didn't before and she definitely won't now," said Beldora, staring pensively away.

"No. We'll just have to sneak in when she's sleeping and find the wand."

Beldora squeezed the bridge of her nose. "You know it won't be that easy. Nothing is."

"How hard can it be to steal a wand from a young girl?" said Bella.

"She's eighteen now. Besides, we couldn't get it from her before. What makes you think this time it will be any easier?"

"Things were different. Now her guard is down and we know where to find her."

"Do we?"

"Yes. She's either at her grandmother's cabin or Bayport, caring for Opal."

"That's right. Opal has been released from the crazy-house," said Beldora. "I'd forgotten."

Bella checked the time. "It's almost ten. I doubt Willow is sleeping just yet."

"Probably not, which is fine with me. I can fit in my show before we go after the wand. Let's meet back here at midnight."

"Okay."

Both women turned back to the globe. "Did you hear that, Vivian?" said Beldora loudly. "We'll be back in a couple of hours."

Vivian's smile was chilly and her eyes hard, but she waved goodbye.

"She's angry again, isn't she?" remarked Bella softly, as she grabbed her shawl and wrapped it around her shoulders.

Beldora grunted. "Do you even have to ask?"

"Tell me again – why are we doing this?" whispered Bella.

"So she can kill Semora and we can get back into our coven."

"Is it worth it?"

"I hope so," replied Beldora, wrapping a thick, wool scarf around her neck. "And I don't see what other choice we have at this point." She glanced back at the globe and felt a niggling of fear in the pit of her stomach.

"What's wrong?" asked Bella, noticing the way the other witch's lips had pursed together.

"Nothing," she replied, forcing a smile back onto her face. She grabbed her broom. "See you back here at midnight?"

"Yes."

The two witches took one last glance toward the globe and then went their separate ways.

CHAPTER FOUR

Kala

"What should we do?" asked Kendra.

"*You* will do nothing," replied Adrianne, removing another tissue from her pocket. She blew her nose and threw it into a nearby wastebasket. "Kind of like my cold medicine."

My sister's eyes widened. "What do you mean? We have to get the globe back before someone finds a way to free her."

Adrianne gave her a reassuring look. "Relax. Vivian can't be released. Not unless someone gets their hands on Juniper or Penelope."

"They're not getting my wand," said Willow firmly.

"Nor mine," I said, touching my hand to it protectively.

"That's right. They won't. Because we're going to hide you *and* the wands," replied Adrianne.

I felt a shiver go down my spine. "*Hide* us? Where?"

"Hey, they could stay at our place in Vail," suggested Tyler, who was drawing squiggles on a notepad.

"That's nice of you to offer but I have something else in mind," said Adrianne. "There's a girl's school in Canada. It's for witches."

I looked at Kendra, who obviously shared my lack of enthusiasm.

"Are you talking about The Roix?" asked Tyler, looking up.

Adrianne nodded. "Yes. All three of you," her eyes moved from me, to Kendra, and then to Willow, "shall go there to stay out of sight and… in the process, learn how to become a more effective witch."

"Can't we just read a manual?" I asked, half joking. "I mean, there must be one, right? Or maybe a book, like *'Witchcraft for Dummies'* instead? I seriously do not want to go to a witch's school."

Adrianne chuckled. "Oh, I'm sure there are many ridiculous books out there, but they're all crap. What this school can teach you won't be found on the Internet or even a book store."

"But we have books like that," I argued. "At Bea's."

"Even so. You need to learn hands-on what it's like casting different spells in a secure environment, Kala."

"Can't you just teach us?" asked Kendra.

"I could teach you some things, but it would be nothing like what the experts at The Roix could. Not only that, you'll learn how to get in touch with the true magical power that's within each of you. The kind that doesn't require a wand or other enchanted item."

"Well, I'm not going anywhere," said Willow firmly. "I can't leave my mother to go off to some school."

"Don't worry, Willow. I'll watch over your mother," said Adrianne, her face softening as she looked at Opal. "She can stay with me while you're gone. It will give us a chance to get to know each other."

"Yes. I would like that," said Opal, looking over at Willow. "Honey, it's important that you learn everything you can about magic."

"But Grams already taught me so much," protested Willow.

"She may have taught you what she knew," said Adrianne. "But, your grandmother lived a very sheltered life. Magic has come a long way and you'll learn things that not even myself, Clarice, or Rebecca could ever teach you."

"She's right," said Opal. "I've heard about that place. You need to go, Willow. At The Roix you'll hone your magical skills and become a very powerful witch. All three of you will."

Willow looked unsure. "But why? I already have a powerful wand. What more do I need?"

Adrianne raised her hand and a ball of light appeared above it. "As I've mentioned before, a wand is not the only way to create magic, my dear." She reached into the light and pulled out a dagger. "It's also not the only way to defend yourself."

Willow's eyes widened.

"I guess we can't argue with that," mumbled Kendra.

"Did you go to a witch school?" I asked Mom.

Adrianne shook her head. "No, but it took me a long time to learn how to draw upon my own powers. There are still many things that I don't know, which is another reason why I'd like you to attend."

My mind was racing. The idea of going to a school specializing in magic sounded exhilarating, and yet, I didn't want to leave Bayport. Not right now. "This is crazy. For one, we can't leave our school. We're graduating this year," I said. "For another, why would we be any safer there? If anything, I think we'd be easier targets."

"Don't worry, when I'm done with you, nobody will recognize you," said Adrianne with a little smile.

"You're going to change our appearances?" asked Kendra, frowning.

"Yes. Girls, to be honest, I don't think you'll have to be away for very long anyway. Once we locate the globe and get things under control, you can decide if you'd like to stay at the school or return home," said Adrianne.

Kendra looked as worried as I felt. "I don't like the idea of leaving Bayport. Besides, they won't be looking for me. They'll be after Kala and Willow. Maybe I could stay behind?"

"I'm not going if you're not," I said firmly.

"You have to stick together," said Tyler, putting a hand on Kendra's shoulder. "You need to watch each other's backs. They're both going to need you and you'll never forgive yourself if something happens and you weren't around to help."

She sighed. "You're right."

"What about our wands?" asked Willow. "They're one-of-a-kind. Someone will recognize at least one of them, won't they?"

"Agreed. They must be kept out of sight," said Adrianne.

"Won't we be expected to have some kind of wand?" I asked, my stomach filling with dread. It seemed like this was a done deal already. Even Kendra looked resigned to the fact that we were going.

"Yes. We'll find you some other wands to use while you're there," she replied.

"What about *our* school?" I asked.

"I'll take care of that," she replied. "As I said earlier, you might only be gone for a few days. You can make up the schoolwork. In fact, I'll talk to your teachers and we'll work something out."

"A few days? What if you don't find the globe?" I asked.

"I'm confident we'll find it. In fact, Clarice should be arriving back here any minute from Oregon," said Adrianne, checking her watch. "She had to cut her trip short and isn't very happy."

"None of us are happy," I mumbled.

"I know. I'm sorry," said Adrianne softly.

"So, when are we supposed to go to this school?" asked Willow.

"Right away. In fact, as soon as Clarice shows up here, we're going to change your appearances and then she's going to escort you to the school," said Adrianne.

Kendra and I looked at each other and groaned.

CHAPTER FIVE

Kala

"Seriously? *Now*?" asked Willow, looking like she wanted to throw up. "You've got to be kidding. It's too soon."

"On the contrary. It might not be soon enough," said Clarice as she materialized next to Tyler. "We don't know who's stolen the globe, and if it's Semora and her coven, then they'd certainly outnumber us at the moment."

"But, they don't want Vivian back," replied Willow. "They even kicked out Bella and Beldora from the coven because they still support her."

"They did?" asked Clarice, her eyebrow raised.

"Yes. I'm surprised you haven't heard," said Kendra. "They've been banned throughout the region. Nobody will take them in. At least that's what Meredith said."

Clarice looked at Adrianne. "Well, then it's pretty obvious – Bella and Beldora took the globe. They're banished and furious about it."

Adrianne nodded. "Yes, and they probably took Isadora's spell book."

"Oh dear, they have that, too?" asked Clarice, frowning.

"Unfortunately, yes. They broke into my safe. I had both items in there," said Adrianne, sounding stuffed up again. She grabbed another tissue from her coat pocket. "Stupid cold. I don't have time for this."

"Drink some green tea," said Clarice.

"I have been," she replied.

"I've got an elixir in my purse that should clear your cold right up," said the older witch, opening up her satchel.

"Oh good," said Adrianne.

"If we know who has Vivian, then why can't we just go after them now?" I asked, watching as Clarice handed Adrianne a small vial of potion. "Instead of sending us away? Surely, we can handle two witches."

"Believe me, we'll be going after them," said Clarice. "But, they're not complete twits. They'll probably even expect it and set traps. Which is why The Roix is a great idea."

"And let's not forget – the girls will learn a few things," added Adrianne, removing the cap from the potion.

"Definitely. Things that will benefit our coven," said Clarice.

"How much should I take?" asked Adrianne.

"Drink it all," said Clarice. "There's not much in there."

"Okay," she said before pouring it down her throat.

"Is that what we are?" I asked. "A coven?"

"Of course," Clarice replied. "I mean, we're a little unconventional, but still a coven."

Opal cleared her throat. "Actually, we're so much more than that." She looked around the room and her eyes became moist. "We're family."

So is Vivian, said the voice in my head. *Family...*

I shuddered. "Exactly. That horrible woman we trapped in the globe is also family and she wants to destroy all of us," I said tightly.

"Yes, she is part of our family," said Clarice, staring at me with concern. "But you know as well as we do that the sentiment means nothing to her. Not like it does to us."

Nodding, I lowered my eyes. "I know."

Clarice moved closer to me. "Are you okay?"

"Yes. Why?" I asked, looking back up and meeting her eyes.

"Where is your wand?" she asked softly.

I patted my coat pocket. "In here, why?"

"Have you been using it?" asked Clarice.

I shrugged. "Just a little."

Her brows drew together. She turned toward Adrianne. "Adrianne, I suspect that the school will be good for Kala, more than anyone."

I stiffened up. "And why is that?" I asked, feeling defensive.

Clarice turned back and her expression was grave. "Because of your wand."

I sighed. "Not this again."

"If you don't learn how to control Penelope, you're going to find yourself heading down the same path as Vivian."

"For one – I will *never* be anything like her," I snapped, angry that she would say something so cruel. "She's an evil woman. For two – I'm not as naïve as you all seem to think I am."

"It has nothing to do with being naïve," said Adrianne. "The wand's influence is very powerful and it's magic... dangerous. Even to its owner."

"Are you trying to say that Vivian was a good woman before using Penelope?" asked Kendra in disbelief.

"Not exactly. But, she wasn't so hateful. In fact, we were once pretty close," she replied, staring off into the distance. "Believe it or not."

"Yes. I remember. Before your mother died," said Clarice.

"After she claimed Penelope, she was never the same," explained Adrianne. She touched my arm. "And that's why we're so worried about you."

"Well, you needn't be," I said, forcing a smile to my face. "Really. I'm fine and I–"

Before I could finish, two other witches appeared in the shop. Adele and Megan.

"Good. We're not too late," said Adele, smiling at me and Kendra. "You're still here."

"Lucky for us," muttered Megan, who was holding a suitcase and looking sullen.

"No, you're not too late. I just told the girls about it and they're not even packed yet. So, Megan is going to The Roix, too?" asked Adrianne, beaming at them.

"Yes. I've been meaning to send her, and now that this situation has come up, I think it would be good for her to join the girls."

"Yes. A very good idea," said Clarice, nodding. She stared at Megan. "I must say, you don't look very pleased."

"Good observation," said Megan dryly.

"You don't want to go?" asked Adrianne.

"Not really," she said, setting her suitcase down. She yawned. "But I don't have a choice, do I, *Mother*?"

"Gah, you're just mad because you don't want to leave Marcus," replied Adele. She sat down on a stool next to the counter. "She has a crush on this guy in her Art class."

"It's Photography," corrected Megan. "And it's not a crush. We're in love."

"Marcus who?" I asked. "Bakerfield?"

"Yes. We've been talking about opening up a studio after graduation. If I leave Bayport to go to this lame magic school, he might change his mind or find someone else."

"A photography studio?" I asked, surprised. Besides her being a witch, Marcus and Megan were two completely different people. He was a jock who listened to country music and played on the football team. She listened to hardcore punk music and had recently started dressing emo. They were like night and day and it seemed odd that those two were "in love." It made me wonder if she'd casted some kind of spell on him. Not that she wasn't pretty. They were just so... different.

"Yes," she said. "I doubt it will happen now, though."

"Well, if he truly loves you he'll wait for you to get back," said Clarice, her eyes twinkling. "And if he doesn't, then he's not worthy of your love."

"Right," she mumbled, brushing a few strands of purple dyed hair away from her eyes.

"We're not exactly thrilled to be going either," I said. "But Clarice seems to think we won't have to be gone for very long."

"She's right," said Adrianne. "Maybe a week or two."

"Actually, I want Megan to stay there for the rest of the school year," said Adele. "She can take her other classes online. The ones she needs to earn her diploma."

"I can't take the photography class online," said Megan, staring at her in disbelief.

"I'm sure we can work something out with your teacher," said Adele. "Or you can transfer into a class that you can take online."

"I doubt it and... I don't want to change classes," she said, her eyes filling with tears.

Adele sighed. "Megan–"

"You just don't want me to have a love-life," said Megan angrily. "And now that I've met someone, you just can't wait to break us up."

Adele looked embarrassed. "That's not true."

"It is true. Why do I need to go with them?" she asked, waving her hand toward us. "They don't need me. Not when they have their wands and each other."

"You girls need to stick together," said Adele. "As friends. As sisters. As a coven. In fact, someday, all you'll have is each other."

Nobody said anything.

Adele raised her chin proudly. "Don't forget... we *are* the Witches of Bayport; I don't know if you realize the significance of that."

"She's right," said Clarice. "Our reputation is growing and because of that, we're becoming more and more respected in the witch community. Especially after the incident with Vivian. Anyway, back to the school. This will be a good way for the four of you to get to know each other."

"Fine. But, I'm not staying longer than two weeks," said Megan stubbornly. "I mean it. I'm almost eighteen and there is no way you can make me stay someplace I really don't want to be. I'll even run away if I have to."

"Don't run away. That never solves anything," said Clarice.

"I will if she makes me stay," threatened Megan, staring at her mother. "Two weeks. That's all I'm staying for."

Adele let out a ragged breath. "Fine. Two weeks."

Megan's face relaxed. "Thank you."

"Now that everything is settled, we'll need to stop back home and pack a few things before we leave," said Adrianne. "You too, Willow."

She nodded.

Adrianne looked at Opal. "And you should pack, too. The safest place for you is with me. There is no telling what lengths Bella and Beldora will go to in order to get their hands on Willow's wand."

"You think that my mother's life could be in danger?" asked Willow, looking frightened.

"I don't know if her life is in danger, but they might try kidnapping her," said Clarice. "Which is why Adrianne and I will keep a very close eye on her."

"As will I," said Adele. "You have my word."

"Thank you. All of you," said Opal. "For stopping Vivian in the first place and protecting my daughter. I can't thank you enough."

"We're family and there's no 'thanks' needed," said Adrianne, smiling warmly at her.

"You know I'd do the same for you," said Opal.

"Of course," replied Adrianne as the clock struck eleven. "Now, let's meet back here in an hour?"

"Yes," said Willow, grabbing onto Opal's hand. She waved her wand and both of them disappeared.

"We'll need to show Opal how to use a wand, if she doesn't know already," said Adele.

"I've got an extra one, too," said Clarice.

"Did you want to wait here?" Adrianne asked Megan and Adele. "While the girls get packed?"

"Sure," said Adele. "We'll just make ourselves at home."

"Is there a television?" asked Megan, looking around.

"In the back room," said Tyler. "I can get it if you'd like."

"No. That's okay. I'll just play games on my phone," said Megan, smiling at him.

"Okay. Adrianne, what would you like me to do?" asked Tyler.

"What time is your mother supposed to be getting home?" she asked.

"I'm not really sure. I guess that depends on how well the date is going. Hopefully, it will be soon."

"You can accompany us back to our place, if you'd like. Then you'll have a little more time with Kendra before she leaves for the school," said Adrianne.

"Sounds good," he replied.

I glanced over at Kendra, who looked miserable. I knew she'd fallen hard for Tyler and he seemed nice, although a little weird at times. Admittedly, everyone I'd met lately fit into that category. Even Bailey. The fact that he could shift into anything he wanted was both exciting and freaky.

"This is only going to be for a couple of weeks, right?" asked Kendra, staring hard at our mother.

"Hopefully. Maybe even less," she answered, giving her a hopeful smile.

"It had better be," said Megan, looking up from her phone. "Or you're on your own."

"Megan. That's rude," said Adele, scowling.

"I'm not trying to be rude. I'm just being upfront. Just like I said before, two weeks is my limit."

"Mine too," I said boldly. "And if you can't find Vivian by then, Kendra and I will go looking for the globe ourselves, and if we have to, destroy both."

My sister's jaw dropped.

"Don't look at me like that. She tried killing Mom as well as us. She's lucky we didn't try returning the favor," I said.

"Kala, murder isn't something we condone," said Clarice. "It's against everything we believe in."

"What about self-defense?" I asked. "Because if my life is threatened, I'm not going to stand back and allow anyone to hurt me, let alone kill me."

"That's an entirely different thing," said Adrianne. "You know that."

"What I do know is that Vivian has tried killing all of us at one point, and here we are, still at her mercy. If she were dead, then we wouldn't have to turn our lives upside down once again, would we?"

"On the contrary," said Clarice. "When it comes to magic, our world will always be a dangerous place."

"She's right," said Adele, sighing.

"I wish I wasn't. In fact, don't think for a second that Vivian is the only person to fear, child. There will always be someone seeking the power of your wand," said Clarice.

"Which is another reason why I should learn how to use it properly," I said.

"Or destroy it," said Adrianne softly.

"That's not going to happen," I said, pulling it out of my pocket. "Penelope."

The wand began to glow. "How may I serve you?" she asked in a voice that was oddly polite, especially for her.

Adrianne and Clarice looked at each other.

"Take me home," I said, relaxing. "Please."

"As you wish."

"See, I told you. I'm in control," I said to my mother, just before disappearing. Unfortunately my satisfaction was short-lived because I materialized into a place that I didn't recognize. Someone's, cold, dark cellar.

CHAPTER SIX

Kala

"Penelope," I scolded, looking around in the darkness. It was damp and smelled like rotting potatoes. "I told you to take me *home*."

The wand laughed mischievously. "Oh, you didn't specify *which* home you meant. Mine or yours."

"But... this isn't your home," I said, looking down at my wand.

"On the contrary. This is where I was created," replied the wand. "It will always be my first home."

"Are you telling me that this is Isadora's cellar?" I asked, now intrigued.

"Yes."

"Illuminate," I said, raising the wand. The fact that we were in the home of such a powerful and notorious witch was both chilling and wondrous.

The room lit up, and as my eyes adjusted to the light, I noted with disappointment that there wasn't anything very special about the cellar. In fact, it was basically empty, save for an old broom that was leaning against a wall. I walked over to it and was about to touch the handle when Penelope ordered me to stop.

"What's wrong?" I asked, pulling my hand back.

"This was Isadora's favorite broom. It might be cursed."

"Might be?"

"Okay. More than likely it's cursed to the gills," she said. "Obviously, touching it would be quite deadly if that's the case."

I took a few steps back, now wanting to get as far from the broom as possible. "No surprise there. Well, thanks for the warning."

"On the other hand," she went on, "if it's not, or the curse doesn't affect you, the broom would be quite a treasure."

"In other words, it would be something worthy of the both of *us*?" I asked dryly.

"Very much so, young witch. Everything Isadora used or created was exceptional. In spite of what it looks like, I guarantee you there isn't a better broom than this. At least not in Salem or... Bayport."

I bit the corner of my lower lip. "But, if I touch it, I could die?"

"It's a risk that might be worth taking."

I grunted. "Easy for you to say."

"Not really. Your death would not be in my best interest."

"Because you like me?" I asked with sarcasm.

"I'm a wand. I have no feelings," she replied. "At least not in the same way that you do. I am a good judge of character, however, and sense that we are good for each other."

"I agree and that's why I want to live."

"You must realize that I wouldn't deliberately put your life at risk."

"As much as I believe that, it still doesn't make me want to take such a chance with it, Penelope," I replied, staring at the broom. It really didn't look like anything special, but knowing that it had been Isadora's was fascinating.

Penelope was quiet for a few seconds and then began to glow again. "Bring me closer and I'll tell you for sure if there's a curse on it or not."

"You can do that?" I asked, wondering why she hadn't mentioned it in the very beginning.

"I can try. Sometimes a curse can be hidden so well, it can't be detected by anyone or anything."

"So, even if you don't find anything, and I decide to try taking it, I could still die?" I replied frowning.

"Mustn't worry about something that hasn't happened yet. Now, bring me closer."

I did what she asked.

"Now, say the word 'Awaken'."

I did and watched as the broom began to sparkle. Penelope became silent.

"Anything?" I asked, after a few seconds. I almost expected the broom to grow a set of arms and then go in search of a water bucket.

"I believe it's safe," she replied.

"You believe?" I said.

"Yes. I sense the magic radiating inside of the broom and there doesn't seem to be anything suppressing it."

"Suppressing it? I don't understand."

"Usually when there's a curse, I am able to sense two separate origins of magic lurking inside the enchanted item. One that belongs there and another that doesn't."

"Hmm, and you only felt one?"

"Yes."

"Should I take it?"

"That's a decision you need to make for yourself."

"Thanks," I said dryly. "You're so helpful."

"Actually, I've been *more* than helpful," she said testily. "Most witches learn everything on their own."

Which is probably why I should go to that school, I thought to myself.

Kala, take the broom.

My eyes widened.

"Did you say something?"

"No," replied Penelope.

So, the voice in my head was back.

It won't hurt you. Take it.

"Speaking of other witches," I said, looking down at my wand. "Do you know if any of them have ever heard voices in their heads?"

"Voices?"

"Yes."

"I'm a wand, not a therapist," said Penelope wryly. "I have no idea."

Take it and get back to your mother. She's worried about you.

Crap.

My mother.

I'd already been gone too long.

Swallowing, I reached my hand toward the broom and said a silent prayer.

CHAPTER SEVEN

Vivian

"Do you think they'll really get us out of here?" asked Mark, sitting across from Vivian. They'd just been served tasteless hamburgers from a waitress named Annie.

Vivian dropped her burger onto the plate. "I hope so. The food here is horrendous and the people... I'd rather be buried under twenty feet of snow than have to deal with these brainless androids for another day."

As if on cue, Annie, returned to the table. "Can I get you more coffee?" she asked with a wide smile and blank stare.

"No," said Vivian, pushing the cup away. "It looks and tastes like muddy water. It's hideous."

"Would you care for dessert or anything else?" Annie asked, oblivious to Vivian's rudeness.

"Do you have any salt?" asked Mark.

"Yes. It's right there," said Annie, nodding toward the shaker.

"Don't bother, Mark. It too has no taste. Just like everything else in this restaurant," said Vivian miserably.

"Would you like me to get you a piece of pie? The apple is to die for," said the waitress.

"I'm sure death would be more tasteful than the crap you're serving," said Vivian.

Annie looked puzzled but then smiled again. "We have cake. Would you like a piece?"

Vivian leaned her forehead down and pretended to hit it against the table. "I really don't know how much more of this I can take."

"It's kind of funny. You have to admit," said Mark.

"Your sense of humor has been tainted by this dreadful globe," said Vivian.

"Any last requests before I get your bill?" asked Annie.

"Actually, yes I do. How about this?" said Vivian, picking up a butter knife. "Shove this into your eyeball. Is that possible?"

Annie blinked and then gave her an apologetic smile. "We don't serve that here, I'm sorry."

"Too bad," said Vivian, stabbing her hamburger with it instead. "It might have actually given me something to smile about today. Let's get out of here, Mark. Before I stab myself in the eye instead."

"Hopefully Bella and Beldora can give both of us something to smile about," said Mark, sliding out of the booth. He looked at his watch. "It's almost midnight, by the way. We should get outside and watch for them."

"Hopefully, neither of the bubbleheads have fallen asleep," said Vivian, standing up.

"Oh, you're leaving? Have a nice day," said Annie as she began clearing away their dishes.

"I'm sorry, but I've got to do this." Mark reached over and touched Annie's cheek. It felt like cool marble. "Weird." He pulled his hand away. "She's like a living doll."

"She's not *living*. It's more like she's pretending to live," said Vivian. "Like we've been doing the past couple of months. Which is why we've got to get the heck out of this place."

"Still, it's fascinating. Who created this globe and these beings?"

"Obviously someone with a warped mind and strange sense of humor," said Vivian, zipping up her jacket.

"A wizard?" he asked. Mark had never met one, but was told that they were even more powerful than the great Isadora Jenkins had been.

Vivian shrugged. "Maybe. And who knows... for all we know, we're sitting inside of an empty globe and everything around us is nothing but a figment of our imagination."

"What about the food?" asked Mark, as another waitress walked by, carrying a tray filled with dessert.

"The food must be real, even as tasteless as it is," replied Vivian. "We've been locked in here for three months and neither of us seem to be dying of hunger."

"Three months already," repeated Mark, sighing. "How long do you think they meant to trap us here for?"

Vivian snorted. "How *long*? Eternity, fool. You didn't think that this was some kind of a time-out, did you?"

He shrugged.

Vivian walked out of the diner, ignoring the cashier who wished her 'a good night' and stepped into the darkness. Unfortunately, where the food was tasteless and the people fake, the chill in the air was real enough. So was the snow.

"Looks like they're not back yet," noted Mark, stepping outside next to her.

"No," she replied, pulling the hood of her jacket over her hair. "Give them time. Something tells me they need us almost as much as we need them."

"Why do you say that?"

"Just a feeling I have."

"Do you think Adrianne might be with them?"

"Possibly. My sister isn't stupid. When she finds out that this globe and the spell book are both missing, she'll question those who were closest to me and those two will break under pressure."

"Do you think she'd send them here with us?"

"Probably, which is another reason we need to get out of here. Those two are our only hope, and if they get imprisoned here with us, we'll all be trapped together for eternity."

There was a flash of light from beyond the globe.

"Ah, looks like they're back," said Vivian pasting on a smile as she waved to the other witches. "Cross your fingers. These two are our only hope now. If they botch this up, neither of us will ever see the light of day again."

**

"So, we're really going to do this?" whispered Bella, ten minutes after checking in with Vivian and Mark. They were standing behind Willow's grandmother's place. As luck would have it, the spell, which had hidden the shabby, weathered cabin from them before, was no longer active.

"We're going to try, although... it looks like nobody is home," answered Beldora, peeking into one of the windows. The lights were out and it was almost impossible to see anything inside. "Maybe they really have abandoned this place, once and for all?"

"That would explain why we were able to locate the cabin so easily this time."

"I'm going in. You keep watch out here."

"Okay," replied Beldora.

Bella waved her wand. She disappeared, and seconds later, materialized into the living room.

"Impressive," she remarked, feeling as if she'd stepped into another dimension.

The interior of the cabin looked like a brand-new, contemporary two-story house. It was gorgeous and looked like something one might see in a home interior magazine. Trendy furniture, newer appliances, and expensive built-ins created, obviously, by magic. Even the ceilings stood much taller than what the exterior hinted at from the outside.

"I need to find out what kind of spells she's been using on this shack," Bella said to herself as she ran a hand over the dark granite island. The kitchen was nothing short of a gourmet and Bella's stomach knotted up with jealousy.

"Wow, who would have known. This place is incredible," said Beldora.

Gasping, Bella turned around and glared at the other witch. "You scared me half to death. Didn't I tell you to stay outside and keep watch?"

"Yes, but I heard something in the woods. I think it might have been a bear." Staring past Bella, her eyes widened. "Is that an espresso maker?"

Beldora was terrified of bears. A few weeks back a couple of raccoons had tipped over her garbage can to get to the leftovers from dinner. The smells had also enticed a hungry black bear, which had surprised her the next morning when she'd stepped onto her porch.

"Yes, it is. Look, there's no reason to be afraid of bears or any other animals, for that matter," said Bella. "You're a witch. You have a wand. Don't be afraid to use it."

"It's not that I'm afraid to use my wand. I just don't want to hurt any animals. I'd rather just avoid them altogether," she replied, looking around nervously. "Anyway, I take it nobody is home?"

"Doesn't look like it."

"Hmm... where do you think Willow is?"

"I don't know. Maybe she and Opal are staying with Adrianne?" said Bella.

"I don't know why they would when this place looks like something you'd see on television."

"Maybe they've found out about the globe being missing already?"

"If so, we could be in trouble."

"I know. I'm beginning to wonder if this is really worth it. Setting Vivian free," said Bella. She was also wondering if it would be better to just keep Juniper for herself, once she got her hands on it. The idea of owning such a powerful wand was very enticing. She might finally get the respect she deserved, too.

"Do you have any better ideas?"

"Not right now. I'm too tired to think," she replied, not knowing if she should share her thoughts with Beldora. They were longtime friends but they'd also had their share of disagreements. Beldora was also much more devoted to Vivian than she.

"Let's head to Bayport and find the wand. Then we'll deal with Vivian later in the day. I don't know about you, but something tells me that if we are able to free her, she's not going to let us rest until she takes revenge on Adrianne and the others. We'll be run ragged," said Beldora.

"We already are running ragged," Bella said, yawning. "I just hope that this is all worth it."

"Hey, whatever it takes to overthrow Semora," said Beldora. "I want that witch put back in her place."

"Me too. It took everything I had not to slap that smug smile from her face when she threw us out. Who does she think she is?"

"We need to knock her off of her high-horse," said Beldora.

"We *could* probably handle it ourselves, you know," Bella asked, testing the waters. "On our own."

She snorted. "Right. If we could do that, we wouldn't be on this scavenger hunt."

"When we get our hands on the wand, we might have the power to do whatever we want," said Bella, watching the other witch closely.

"You need more than the power of the wand," said Beldora. "Anyway, Vivian knows how to use Juniper. We don't."

"We could learn. How hard could it be?"

Beldora frowned.

"Vivian has never used the wand either. She knows about as much as we do," pointed out Bella.

"It doesn't matter. We promised her that we'd free them."

"I know. I'm just saying that if you wanted to handle Semora on our own, I wouldn't be against it. It's not a big deal. I just figured I'd run it past you."

"I'll keep that in mind," replied Beldora. "For now, let's worry about getting our hands on the darn thing."

"Yes. So, where to? Bayport?"

Beldora nodded. "Back to Adrianne's. Let's just hope they haven't figured out that the spell book and globe are missing yet."

"It's late, but you never know. Vivian said that she hadn't seen Adrianne checking on them for a while, so the odds are in our favor. Still, we need to be careful."

"Exactly. We can't underestimate any of them. Vivian did and look where it got her."

Another reason we might not want to free Vivian, thought Bella.

Vivian's obsession with trying to destroy Adrianne had made her reckless and stupid. She certainly didn't want to let her drag them down with her a second time.

Chapter Eight

Kala

"Where have you been?!" demanded Adrianne when I walked through the front door of our house. She stood in the living room with Clarice, both of them looking relieved but ready to throttle me.

I smiled weakly. "Sorry. I had to pick up my broom," I replied, holding it out. "And then test it out. These things go crazy fast, don't they?" My face was still half frozen from the flight.

"Yes," agreed Clarice. "Still my favorite way to travel."

"I can see why," I replied.

In all honesty, I'd been frightened at first, but then knowing that Kendra had flown a few times, I sucked it up and soon found myself enjoying the ride.

"Since when did you get a broom?" asked Adrianne, incredulously. "And who taught you how to fly?"

"Penelope found it for me," I said, turning around. I leaned the broom against the wall and began removing my wet boots. "As for flying, I guess you could say, I taught myself."

"You did? Good for you," said Clarice. "It can be a harrowing experience, especially being alone."

"It was definitely scary, but I figured things out," I said, wanting to prove to them that I wasn't a child anymore.

"Hmm, I've seen this before…" Clarice walked over and began scrutinizing my broom. After a few seconds, she tapped her finger against her chin and nodded. "Yes, it must be hers."

"What do you mean?" asked Mom, her eyebrows knitting together. "Who is *her*?"

Clarice, who wore a shawl, pulled it tighter around her shoulders. "Let's just say that I've seen this broom before. Back in Salem."

"Salem?" repeated Adrianne. "Don't tell me you were in Salem, Kala."

"Okay, I won't tell you," I said, smiling.

"This isn't funny," said Adrianne. "Were you in Salem?"

"Er, yeah. I was," I said.

She gave me a disapproving look.

"I knew I recognized the broom," said Clarice.

"How? It's just a broom. You must have seen dozens in your life," I replied.

To me, it didn't look that much different from any other. The only reason I knew it was special was because of the connection we now had, and our little flight home. When I'd made my decision back at Isadora's to throw caution to the wind and touch the thing, something magical happened between us. The moment my fingers connected with the handle, a surge of warm energy spread into my fingertips and rushed through the rest of my body. As this was happening, I came to the realization that the broom had been in some kind of hibernation – dormant, in fact, waiting for a new owner to take possession, and bring it back to life.

"Normally, no. But, this was Isadora's broom," continued Clarice, pointing to something on the handle. "You see there? She had to repair it after someone tried shooting her out of the sky. You can see where the wood was fused back together."

"Who tried to do that?" I asked, leaning closer to look at where the wood had been reconnected.

"Isadora had a lot of enemies," said Clarice. "When you're that powerful, there are more of those than friends. Speaking of which, how did you end up at her place?"

"Penelope misunderstood my request," I admitted. "And brought me to where she was created."

Adrianne scowled. "And this is why you have to be very careful with that wand, Kala."

"And specific. Especially with the dark wands. They can be crafty and devious. Even to their owners, if they think they can get away with it," said Clarice.

"In this case, she was only trying to help me out. Penelope knew I needed a broom and she found one worthy of us," I said.

"Is that you are the wand talking?" asked Clarice, amused.

I couldn't help but grin back. "Anyway, it's getting late. I'd better go and pack. Unless, you've changed your mind and we're staying?"

"Sorry. No such luck," said Adrianne.

"Are you feeling better?" I asked, noticing that her red nose was gone and the color was back in her face.

"Yes. The potion worked wonders," said Adrianne. "Too bad I hadn't had it earlier, when I was watching the kids."

Thinking of her daycare business, which she'd resumed the month before, I suddenly remembered my promise to Bea. "Oh, my gosh! I told Beatrice that I'd open the bookstore for her tomorrow."

"I'll call and let her know what's happening. I'm sure she'll understand," said Clarice. "And, if she still needs someone in the morning, I'll take care of it."

I sighed in relief. "Thanks. She was asking about you anyway."

"It's been awhile since we've been able to sit down and talk. We grew up together, you know," said Clarice.

"She mentioned that. By the way, where's Kendra?" I asked.

"Upstairs packing and pouting," said Adrianne. "Willow and Opal should be here any minute, so you'd better get a move on."

"Okay. I'll be back down in a few minutes," I said, leaving the living room.

I went upstairs to the bedroom that I still shared with Kendra.

"Hi," she said, zipping up a dark brown luggage bag. Her hair was up and she'd changed into a pair of blue jeans and a black, fuzzy sweater.

"Hi," I replied, moving toward the closet. "You all set?"

"I'm sure I'm forgetting something." Kendra sat down on her bed, looking angry.

"This bites, huh?"

"Tell me about it. I'm so sick of Vivian ruining everything for us. Even confined to that stupid globe, she is still turning our lives upside down."

"I know. It's ridiculous," I replied, pulling out some clothing from my side of the closet. "I still don't understand why we can't just stay here, hold our ground or even go search for Vivian ourselves. Hiding out in some magic school, where we can't even use our wands anyway, just seems like a waste of time."

"They won't let us do that. Mom and Clarice are way too overprotective," she said as I lay some of my shirts onto the bed. "It's so frustrating."

"You can say that again." I went back to the closet and grabbed some more of my tops. "They don't trust us or our judgments. They have no reason not to. We were the ones who saved Mom in the first place. *We* were the ones who trapped Vivian in that globe." I put my hands on my hips and turned to look her, "In fact, I really do think we should go to Salem right now, find Bella and Beldora, and make them give up the globe."

Kendra snorted. "Go to Salem by ourselves? Right," she said dryly. "Look, I'm not happy about this school but there's no way I'm setting foot in Salem, especially without proper backup. And yeah, our wands are pretty awesome, but face it – Bella and Beldora not only have been practicing magic longer than us, they don't fight fair."

"True," I said. Not only that, but their's was also Black magic.

"You two packed yet?" asked a voice.

We both turned to find Willow standing at the doorway. She wore an oversized purple hoodie along with black leggings and suede boots.

"I am. She's just starting," said Kendra. She nodded toward a hot pink saucer chair, sitting in the corner. "Come on in and join us in our ranting."

"Thanks," she replied, shoving her hands into the pockets of her hoodie. She walked in and sat down.

"You okay?" I asked, staring at her. Her long, dark hair was pulled back into a knotted bun, making her cheekbones more pronounced. With her pale skin and haunted brown eyes, she looked more like thirteen than nineteen.

She shrugged. "I'm fine. Just a little freaked out by all of this. I thought the Vivian matter was all taken care of, you know?"

"Yeah, me too. I'm sure it will get resolved quickly, though," said Kendra with a sympathetic smile.

"Let's hope," I replied, pulling clothing out of my dresser drawers. "I swear, things are so crazy. You'd think we'd be getting used to it by now."

"My life has always been pretty unpredictable," said Willow grimly. "Until lately. I should have known it was too good to be true. I swear, whenever my life starts feeling 'normal', something bad happens."

"Nothing bad has happened yet," I reminded her. "I mean, this sucks, yeah. But, hopefully Mom and Clarice will take care of this quickly before there is any real 'bad'."

"I just hate being forced away from my mother again," she replied.

"I know what you mean about being separated," said Kendra. "Tyler and I have been together almost every day. I'm pretty sure he loves me as much as I...." She blushed but didn't go on.

"Love him?" I said with a knowing smile. "It's pretty obvious you two are head-over-heels for each other."

"I suppose. What about you and Bailey? You barely say anything about him," said Kendra. "What's going on between the two of you?"

I shrugged. "I don't know. I think he's hot. He definitely gives me butterflies. I just don't know if it's *love* that I feel," I replied, shoving underwear and socks into my bag.

"Well, like Forrest Gump once said, 'I know what love is' and I definitely love Tyler," said Kendra, laying her head back down on the pillow. She stared up at the ceiling. "And the thought of being away from him for two weeks makes me sick."

"He can visit you though, can't he?" asked Willow, biting a corner of her chipped, purple fingernail.

"Maybe. Mom said it was a bad idea but," she smiled, "we all know that he can control minds and make people forget stuff. So even if he was caught, I can't see what harm it would really do. I'll probably try sneaking him in. Just for a little while."

"I think you'd better reconsider. Even with that kind of power, a person can make a mistake," I said. "What if someone spotted him and you missed it? That could get ugly."

She let out a frustrated sigh.

"I'm telling you, we could take care of this tonight. All three of us. Go after them."

"Go after whom?" asked Willow, leaning forward. "You mean Bella and Beldora?"

"Yes. Get the globe back and destroy it, so we don't have to worry about this ever happening again," I said.

"Are you actually talking about killing Vivian?" asked Kendra, her eyes wide.

"Yes. I guess so. She wants to kill us and if she gets out, you know it's number one on her priority list," I said flatly. "So why not?"

"I'll tell you why not," said Clarice, now standing in the doorway with a disapproving frown.

I cringed. *Crap.*

"First of all, murder is still murder. Not only does it violate the laws of man and our coven, it's against everything Adrianne and I believe in."

I sighed.

"Kala, I'm pretty sure she raised you with the same morals. And second, you said so yourself – you're not anything like Vivian. By taking a life, even a wicked one like hers, you begin a journey down a road that never ends."

"Yes, but, if she finds us, she'll try killing us again," I replied.

"And if she does, you have every right to defend yourself," said Clarice, stepping into the room. "But my dear, if you go searching for trouble, you may find much more than what you or any of us can handle."

"She's right," said Kendra. "I think we're jumping ahead of ourselves, anyway. She's probably still trapped in the globe and we're stressing out about something that will never happen."

Clarice nodded. "You're right. We also don't know for sure who has taken the globe or how many people are involved. That's why you three girls need to get your butts to The Roix and let us handle this."

And what if they can't? They could walk into a trap and you'd never hear from them again, said the voice in my head.

"But, we could help," I replied, ticked that I was still hearing things.

"Your leaving is what helps us the most," said Clarice. "If you're hidden somewhere safely, we can concentrate on the matters at hand and not protecting you. So," she waved her hand toward my luggage, "finish up so we can introduce you to your new identities."

From the stubborn look on her face, I knew that I was wasting my breath.

"Okay," I replied. "Fine. We'll do it your way."

"Thank you," she said.

Kendra, who was staring toward our bedroom window, gasped loudly. She quickly pulled out her wand. "Oh, my God, there's someone out there!"

Startled, I whipped my head around and pulled out my wand. "Who was it?"

"I couldn't tell," she replied, looking pale. "It appeared to be a woman, though."

Clarice aimed her wand toward the window and mumbled something. A bolt of lightning shot out the tip and through the glass, lighting up the sky like it was the Fourth of July.

"Whoa!" said Willow.

Clarice rushed to the window and we followed.

"Is there anyone out there?" I asked, peering over her shoulder.

"I think I saw two women," said Clarice as the sky began to darken and the light receded. Do you think it was Bella or Beldora, Kendra?"

"It might have been Bella," answered Kendra.

"I'm sure it was and that's why we need to get you out of Bayport," said Clarice.

"What's going on?" asked Adrianne, rushing into the room with Opal.

"I think Bella and Beldora were here," said Clarice.

"Oh no. We have to get them out of here," said Adrianne. "They're looking for the wands, obviously."

"Hurry. Get your stuff together," said Clarice. "Now that they know we're here, I think it would be safer to bring the girl's to Rebecca's place in Vail right now, before they leave for the school. In fact, I'll go back to Secrets and round up Adele and Megan, too, so they know what's going on. We'll meet you there."

"Okay," said Adrianne. "Grab your luggage bags, girls."

"Is everything going to be okay?" asked Opal, her face pale.

"Yes, don't worry," said Adrianne, giving her a reassuring smile. "We're bringing the girls to a safe place. Speaking of which, I think you should stay in Vail, too, until everything is worked out. I'm sure Rebecca won't mind."

"No, she doesn't mind at all," said Rebecca herself, walking into the bedroom. "What she does mind is that you're all still here."

"I'm done packing," I said, zipping up my bag. "We can leave."

"Good," said Rebecca. She turned to Adrianne and her eyes softened. "I heard what's happening and I'm so sorry you're having to go through this again."

"We'll be fine," she replied, her smile looking forced. "How can we not be when there are more of the good guys than the bad, right?"

"Exactly," said Tyler, peeking his head into the bedroom. "Which reminds me, I brought another one of the good guys. I didn't think you'd mind."

Bailey walked into the bedroom and our eyes met immediately.

"Oh. Hi," I said, feeling a rush of warmth spread through me. With everything that was happening, I was relieved to see him. He made me feel safe.

"Hope you don't mind but I'm here to help escort all of you ladies to wherever you need to go," said Bailey, puffing out his chest. "So, don't even think about arguing with me."

"We wouldn't dream of it," said Adrianne. "Right, Kala?"

"Of course not," I replied, giving her a hard stare.

She ignored it.

"Good. Could you give me a lift?" he asked. "I mean, I could probably wing it as a bird, but something tells me we're not flying."

"No time to fly," I said, picking up my bag. "And, you can hitch a ride with me."

"I was hoping you'd say that," he replied, walking over to me.

Clarice looked Rebecca. "Do you know where Adele and Megan are?"

"They're downstairs. They followed me here," she answered.

"Good," said Adrianne. She raised her wand. "If you could please let them know what's going on. I've got some things to take care of."

"Where are you going?" asked Kendra.

"Not far. I'll see you soon," she answered before disappearing.

"I wish she wouldn't do that," said Kendra sternly.

"I know. She hates it when we do it," I said.

"Your mother will be fine," said Rebecca. "Don't worry."

Kendra sighed deeply. "How can I not worry? For all we know, Vivian has found a way out of the globe."

"If she did, we'd know it by now," said Tyler.

"And she'd be the one stalking us," I added, walking over to the window again. I looked outside and the hair on the back of my neck stood up. They were out there. Watching and waiting for their chance to take my wand. Or Willow's. I would never let that happen.

"Let's go," said Clarice. "It's not safe here."

"Kala?" said Bailey, now standing next to me. "You okay?"

"Yes," I replied, looking up to him. "Are you ready to go?"

He grabbed my hand and slid his fingers between mine. "For you, I'm always ready. Now, let's get you to safety, little witch."

I smiled and waved my wand.

CHAPTER NINE

Bella

"They were *all* in there?" asked Beldora, as the two witches hurried across the street from Adrianne's home.

Bella looked back up toward the bedroom, where she could see Clarice's ample form now in the window. "Yes."

"Then they obviously know."

"Obviously," she said, as they took cover behind the neighbor's tall bushes.

"Could you hear what they were saying?"

Bella stared at the house, wondering if they should just go back to Salem, or try stealing the wand. They'd come so far and it would be a shame to give up now. Vivian would demand that they return anyway. "Part of it. Something about The Roix."

A dog began to bark. It sounded like a small yipping one. "Darn it," said Beldora. "Noisy dog."

Bella raised her wand, whispered a few words, and the dog yipped but then became silent.

Beldora raised a hand to her mouth in horror. "You didn't hurt it, did you?"

"Don't worry about the dog right now. Worry about us," scolded Bella. "And whether they saw us or not."

"You think they did?"

"Probably. Let's go," said Bella, grabbing the other witch's arm.

"I've heard of The Roix," said Beldora, letting Bella lead her away. "Isn't that an exclusive place for witches?"

"I'm not sure how exclusive it is if they're allowing vermin like them in," said Bella, although she knew that Adrianne was well respected in the witch community. Especially after what had happened with Vivian. The school probably sent them personal invitations.

"Do you think they're going there?"

"I believe so. I couldn't hear that much," she whispered. "Just move your butt. I'm sure they're looking for us."

Beldora glanced behind them. "Great," she muttered.

"Quickly. This way," Bella said, heading toward a back alley.

She followed her, wincing at the pain in her side. "I have to stop. It hurts."

"You really need to get more exercise," said Bella, who was normally up at the crack of dawn most mornings, jogging. She'd been trying to get Beldora to join her, but the woman had an aversion to physical activity, unless it involved running out for pizza.

"Don't tell me something I already know," said Beldora, trying to keep up. "You know that bad knees run in my family, right? It limits me."

Always the excuses, thought Bella. "You're going to have more than bad knees if we're caught," she said, still moving at a brisk pace.

"Hold up. I can't do this anymore," panted Beldora, stopping now to catch her breath.

Bella stopped and turned around. At least they were out of Adrianne's neighborhood.

"Why don't we just go back to Salem?" asked Beldora, holding her side as she caught up.

"We can't. We have to get one of those wands. Besides, that's the first place Clarice and Adrianne will look for us."

"Maybe nobody recognized you."

"I'm not taking any chances."

"So what do you suggest?" she asked irritably. "I'm not sure how much longer I can keep going. I hadn't planned on being up all night, you know."

"Neither had I," said Bella wearily. "We need to figure out something though. And quickly."

Beldora, chewing on her lower lip, suddenly had another idea. "If Kala is going to The Roix, why don't we just take Penelope from her there? We could figure out a way to sneak in, you know?"

Bella nodded slowly. "Actually, that might not be a bad idea. In fact, an old friend of mine works at The Roix. Sybil Hotchkins."

Beldora's face brightened. "She does? Uh, who is Sybil Hotchkins?"

"I'm surprised you don't know who I'm talking about. We went to high school together. Her cousin was on the football team and everyone had a crush on him."

"Sorry, it's just not ringing a bell."

"It doesn't matter," she replied. Beldora was notoriously absentminded. "I think I heard that she teaches Potions, from Greta Fairfaith."

"Oh, I know her."

"I'd hope so. She's your cousin," said Bella dryly.

Beldora blushed.

"Anyway, it's been years since we've spoken, but Sybil still owes me a favor. A big one. I bet she can tell me if the girls have enrolled into the school."

Beldora's eyes lit up. "Wait a second. I *do* remember Sybil. She and her brother even grew up down the street from me. But, she's a white witch isn't she?"

"Yes."

"Why does *she* owe *you* a favor?"

"Let's just say that Sybil once needed an antidote after experimenting with a potion that nearly killed her. Fortunately for her, I had what she needed."

"Really? What was that?"

"Dragon marrow."

Beldora's eyes widened. "How in the world did you get your hands on *that*?"

"My mother had it. She paid a lot of money for the marrow, though, and wasn't too happy at the time. Anyway, if I hadn't given some of it to Sybil, she wouldn't be breathing, let alone teaching anywhere."

"Excellent. Do you think Sybil will help us though?"

"Yes, as long as she doesn't know our true motives."

Beldora bit the side of her lip. "What are you going to tell her?"

Bella was quiet for a few seconds and then she smiled. "I'm going to ask that she help my niece get into the school."

"But you don't have a niece."

She smiled and raised her wand. "I do now."

Beldora's eyes widened. "Don't... you... dare..."

Bella concentrated on a spell that would take off twenty years. "Sorry, Bel. What other choice do we have?" she said, before zapping her with the wand.

The other witch groaned. "What if she recognizes me?"

"I doubt she'll remember you from twenty years ago." And it wasn't like Beldora was popular in school. Not like Sybil and her hunky cousin.

"Why can't you just tell her that your niece couldn't make the tour? You know how much I hate this," she said, looking down at herself in dismay.

"Because it would raise suspicion," said Bella, staring at a teenaged version of Beldora. "Anyway, you should be thrilled that you're a teenager again. I must say, I like your hair better this length. And you've got your girlish figure back."

"True," said Beldora, touching her brown hair. She grimaced. "What have you done to my hair?"

"It's a pixie cut," said Bella, admiring her work. "It's adorable."

"I don't care. Make it longer."

"But, this is the 'in' style right now. You look perky and cute."

"I don't care about being perky and cute, I'm not an elf. At least give me a bob," she demanded.

Bella rolled her eyes. "Fine."

Seconds later, Beldora had a bob and was checking her reflection in a small compact mirror. "Much better. Goodness, where have the years gone?"

"Ed took them from you," reminded Bella. Ed was her dead husband. The one who'd cheated on Beldora one too many times. He was now resting in 'pieces' behind his old toolshed.

Beldora's face darkened. "Don't say that swine's name again."

"Sorry," said Bella, taking out her cell phone.

Beldora put the mirror away. "Are you sure this is even going to work?"

"It has to," Beldora replied, sending Sybil a text.

"What has to?" asked a voice in the darkness.

Both witches gasped and turned around. Adrianne's resemblance to Vivian was enough to make both of them look twice.

"What has to?" repeated Adrianne.

"Adrianne?" asked Bella.

Adrianne smiled coldly. "Yes. Who did you expect? Vivian?"

"Uh, no," said Bella, trying to remain calm. "That wouldn't be possible, right?"

"You tell me," she replied.

Bella and Beldora looked at each other.

"Cat got your tongues?" Adrianne asked.

"No," said Bella. "Not at all."

"Then tell me, what are you two doing out here, in the middle of the night, and in my neck of the woods?" asked Adrianne sharply.

Beldora, looking like a deer caught in someone's headlights, took a step back. "Uh, we were looking..."

"For Rebecca," finished Bella. "We need something from her store."

"Funny, her 'store' isn't anywhere near my house," said Adrianne, almost amused that they were trying so hard.

"We followed her from Secrets," said Bella quickly. "We know she's at your place."

"So, why didn't you come to my front door?" asked Adrianne.

"We know that we're not welcome at your place," said Bella, "because of the allegiance we had before to your sister."

"Yes, there is that," mused Adrianne. "Anyway, why couldn't this wait until the morning when the store is open?"

"It's an emergency," replied Beldora. "We were hoping to talk to her when she left your home."

Adrianne eyed her curiously. "I see. My, my. What are you up to, Beldora? Looking like a teenager again?"

Beldora blushed. "Uh, yes. It's Bella's idea of a joke."

"Very amusing. What isn't, is that it's late and you two are obviously up to something," said Adrianne.

"I told you... we need something from Rebecca's store," said Bella firmly.

"What do you need?" asked Adrianne, not believing a word of it. "Maybe I can help you."

"And why would you do that?" asked Bella.

"Unlike my sister, I can be reasonable," she replied.

"Fine. If you must know, we need extra protection from Semora and the coven," said Bella. "You heard that they banished us, didn't you?"

"Yes, but why would you need protection from them?" asked Adrianne.

"Semora wants us dead," said Bella.

"That's a little extreme," admitted Adrianne.

"You could say that again," said Bella.

Adrianne stared at her hard. "Don't you think you're overreacting? I've heard Semora has always been fair and murder doesn't sound anything like her."

"Forgive *me*, but you have no idea what goes on in the coven," said Bella stiffly. "And what she's capable of."

"True. I don't. Nor do I really want to." Adrianne's eyes bore into hers. "But one thing I do know is that your ties to my sister still run deep and finding you snooping around in my neighborhood does not make me happy."

"Rest assured, we have no more ties to your sister," said Bella, forcing a smile to her face. "And we've told Semora that as well. But, she doesn't believe us."

"Neither do I," said Adrianne. "Which is why I'm going to have to ask you to leave. Immediately."

"Fine. You don't have to be so rude about it," said Bella, her cheeks reddening.

"Don't get me started on being rude," said Adrianne giving her a scalding look.

"Let's go," said Beldora.

"You know, your sister was right about you," said Bella glaring at her. "You think you're so much better than everyone else."

"You're speaking of the wrong sister and I think both of you know that. To Vivian, nothing else matters in this world but power and she'll step on anyone or anything to get it."

Neither witch said anything.

Adrianne gave them a stern look. "Heed my warning – don't do anything reckless for my sister. No matter what happens, you'll get hurt in the end."

"Are you threatening us?" asked Bella, her eye twitching.

"No. I'm trying to warn you, but..." Adrianne smiled coolly. "Like you said – you have no more ties to Vivian."

"That's right," said Beldora. "We don't. Come on, Bella," said Beldora, grabbing the other witch's arm.

Adrianne, knowing that the two of them wouldn't admit to stealing the globe and spell book, decided to put it out there anyway. "One more thing – I'm missing something of great importance. You wouldn't happen to have seen it?"

"That depends. What is it that you're missing?" asked Bella wide-eyed.

"Believe me, you'd know it if you saw it," replied Adrianne.

"Not one of the girls' bonding wands?" asked Bella, putting a hand to her chest.

"No," said Adrianne, inwardly rolling her eyes. "Those are where they should be."

"Is it a magical item?" asked Bella, feigning ignorance.

"Yes," said Adrianne, playing the game. "Two items, in fact."

"Oh, come now. You have to give us more than that," said Bella.

"Let's just say both of the missing items are... family heirlooms and I will do *whatever* it takes to get them back," she replied firmly.

"Well, good luck," said Beldora, pulling at Bella's arm again. "Come on. Let's go home, Bella."

"Yes. Good luck finding what it is you're looking for, Adrianne," said Bella.

"Thank you. I have a good idea of where they might be, so it won't be long now," said Adrianne.

The two witches looked at each other and then disappeared.

Torn between wanting to follow the troublemakers and returning to Kendra and Kala, Adrianne chose the latter. She didn't have time to go on a wild goose chase and something told her that Bella and Beldora weren't stupid enough to lead her back to Vivian. She also didn't want to face them alone. Not in Salem. It was always possible that those two witches weren't working alone. She decided that after Clarice returned from The Roix, they would confront them together. Maybe even bring in Meredith or Semora if needed.

Releasing a ragged sigh, she waved her wand and headed to Vail.

CHAPTER TEN

Kala

"Did you find them?" I asked Adrianne when she finally appeared. We were in Rebecca's kitchen, drinking coffee and discussing our new identities. I was going to be a redhead with brown eyes and killer cheekbones named Sara Fender, daughter of Bernie and Mary. They were "currently" on some kind of a church mission in Africa, along with Kendra's faux parents. She was to be my cousin, Jane Fender. Megan and Willow would be stepsisters from Sweden, their parents were also on the same mission. Fortunately, Clarice was good friends with the dean of the school, Marigold Weiss, who would know our true identities, and back up our stories. Apparently, Marigold despised Vivian and was willing to do whatever it took to keep her from escaping the globe.

"Oh, yes," said Adrianne, pushing her hair away from her eyes. "I snuck up and gave them half a fright, too."

"Good," said Clarice. "What did they say?"

Adrianne removed her jacket. "They lied and said they were looking for Rebecca."

"Really? They said they were looking for *me*?" asked Rebecca, looking amused. "What was their reasoning?"

"Apparently, they wanted to purchase something that would kill Semora," said Adrianne. "Before she gets to them first. They claim that she wants to murder them."

"I think we all do at this point," said Clarice dryly.

"Do you think Semora is really trying to do that?" asked Willow.

"No. It's just a bunch of hogwash the two of them are using. An excuse to be in Bayport," said Adele, who was sitting at the kitchen table and paging through The Roix School's pamphlet. She looked over her shoulder at Adrianne. "We all know that if Semora wanted them dead, she would have done it by now."

"You should probably fill Aunt Semora in on what's happening," said Megan. "She'd get a kick out of all this."

"Already did. She's going to help us search for the globe and spell book."

"Good. Then maybe we won't have to stay very long at The Roix," said Megan, looking relieved.

"Hopefully that will be the case," said Kendra.

"I know that you're not happy about going, but you'll be thanking your mothers later. The Roix is a very prestigious magic school and you might learn a lot, even in the few days you'll be attending," said Rebecca.

"Don't say 'few days'," muttered Megan. "Say 'few hours'. Please."

"With an attitude like that, you're not even going to give it a chance," stated Adele, putting the pamphlet down. "You need to lighten up, dear. This will be good for you."

"Right," said Megan, twirling her stir stick in the cup of coffee.

"Speaking of the school, we should get going," said Clarice, nodding toward the clock in the kitchen. It was almost three a.m. "I told Marigold we'd be arriving soon. She's waiting for us. If we don't leave now, it will border on being rude."

I glanced at Bailey, who was sitting next to me silently, a pensive look on his face. We'd filled him in on everything and he'd immediately volunteered to search for the globe and spell book. Clarice had suggested that he accompany us to The Roix instead. He'd agreed, admitting that our safety should be first priority anyway.

"Okay, girls," said Adrianne. "It's time to change into your new personas."

"How will that be done? Is it some kind of spell?" I asked, feeling a little excited.

Clarice picked up her satchel and started digging inside. "No. A doppelganger potion from Haiti. I picked some up at the convention. Good thing I did."

"How long does this potion last?" asked Kendra. "It's not permanent, is it?"

My sister had taken a potion, which had slimmed her down just a couple of months before. She hadn't regained any of her weight back but that could have been due to a number of other reasons, as well.

"No. Not at all. In fact, these potions will only last for a maximum of twenty-four hours. So, you'll need to keep taking more every couple of days or until we can bring you home," she replied, pulling out a large, brown bottle. "Rebecca, do you have the images?"

"Yes," she said, holding up pictures from a teen magazine. "The girls have each chosen their new look."

We'd each been allowed to select a photo of one of the models in the magazine, which admittedly, had actually been fun. Especially knowing that we'd look like their identical twin.

"Excellent," said Clarice, setting the bottle down on the counter. "Could you get us four glasses of water, Adrianne? We'll need about six ounces in each one. No more. No less."

"Yes," Rebecca said, walking to the cupboard. She did what Clarice asked, measuring the water carefully, and then set each glass down on the counter.

"Good. Now, we'll need to tape each picture around one of the glasses, photo side facing the inside of the glass," instructed Clarice.

"I'll help," said Tyler, grabbing some tape from one of the kitchen drawers.

When that was finished, Clarice opened up the bottle of doppelganger potion. "Now, watch carefully so you know what to do when you're at the school and need to do this yourselves."

We all gathered around the glasses and watched as Clarice added two drops of the potion into each one carefully. As soon as the magical liquid hit the water, it began to bubble.

"When the bubbles have subsided, you will each take the glass with the picture of your chosen identity and drink it down," said Clarice. "Every last drop."

"Is it nasty?" asked Megan, frowning.

"I have no idea. I've never used it before," said Clarice.

"How do you know that it actually works?" asked Willow, looking unsure.

"It will work," she replied. "I paid a lot of money for it. It has to."

"I'll pay you back," said Adrianne. "And girls, don't worry. It will work. I've tried a doppelganger potion before."

"When?" I asked her.

"Back when you were babies and I needed a disguise," she replied, picking up the bottle of potion. She removed the stopper from the top and sniffed the bottle. "Well, this smells exactly as I remembered it."

"That bad, huh?" asked Kendra.

"No. It smells like lemon, actually," she replied, putting the cap back onto the bottle.

"Girls, get ready," said Clarice, bending over the glasses. "The bubbles are beginning to subside already."

I looked into my glass and watched as the liquid calmed.

"Well, here goes nothing," said Megan, picking up her glass. I watched as she drank it down quickly and then set the glass back on the counter.

"Quickly. Drink your potions," said Clarice, nodding toward the rest of us.

Taking a deep breath, I picked up my glass and began drinking the liquid down. There wasn't much of a taste, just a hint of lemon and something that reminded me of grass. When I was finished, I set the glass back down on the counter and watched Kendra and Willow do the same.

"I don't think it's working," said Megan, looking down at her arms and torso. "I don't feel anything."

"Give it time," said Adrianne. "It can take a few minutes."

"Uh, actually, I am beginning to feel something and it isn't good," said Megan, clutching her stomach with a grimace. She gave Clarice a horrified look. "I feel sick to my stomach."

Rebecca pointed toward the hallway. "The bathroom is down there."

"Okay," said Megan.

"Great," I mumbled, my own tummy starting to feel funny. "I'm nauseous, too. Is this supposed to happen?"

"You'll be fine," said Adrianne. "Just wait."

Megan put a hand to her mouth and burped loudly. Then she looked at us, a relieved expression on her face. "Sorry about that."

"It's okay. Do you feel better?" asked Adrianne.

"Yeah, actually," she replied.

"How long is this supposed to take?" asked Willow, her face pale.

"Soon, I hope," said Megan, whose own face was beginning to turn red. "I'm getting very warm. Is that normal?"

Adrianne nodded. "Yes. How are you doing, Kendra? You've been very quiet."

"Lovely," she said dryly.

"I think this was a bad idea," I replied, just before burping. I gave Bailey an apologetic look. "Sorry."

He grinned. "That was impressive. Do you feel any better?"

I actually did. Much better. "Yes."

Willow let out a burp and then laughed. "Talk about weird, huh?"

"It's about to get weirder," said Adrianne. "But you girls will be just fine."

Megan gasped and touched her cheeks.

"Whoa," said Kendra, staring at her.

"What's happening?" squeaked Megan.

I watched in wonder as her skin began to move underneath her fingertips.

"It's happening," said Adrianne, nodding.

My own face grew hot and seconds later, it felt as if the bones under my skin had turned to jelly.

"You might want to sit down," I heard Adrianne say as my legs became wobbly. "All of you."

I sank down to the floor, wanting it to be over with.

It's almost over, said the voice in my head.

"I hope so, Vee," I slurred, deciding to give the voice a name.

"Who is 'Vee'?" asked Adrianne.

The voice in my head, I wanted to say, but my lips would no longer move.

"Hey, are you okay?" asked Bailey, now on his knees next to me.

I stared at him helplessly, now unable to speak. Soon, I couldn't even keep my eyes open.

Don't fight it. Just let go... whispered Vee.

I closed my eyes and was pulled into a calming darkness.

***

"Kala? Can you hear me?"

"Mom?" I whispered hoarsely, opening my eyes.

"Are you okay?" she asked, leaning over me.

"Yeah."

"You were having a nightmare," she said, staring down at me with concern.

"I was?" I said, noticing Bailey on the opposite side of me. "I don't remember anything."

"Good, because it must have been a bad one," she said.

"How do you know?" I asked.

"You were crying in your sleep," said Bailey.

I touched my cheeks and noticed they were wet. I wiped the tears away with the back of my hand. "Oh wow. That's weird. How long was I out for?"

"Just a couple of minutes," Adrianne said. "The others are just waking up now, too."

"Did it work?" I asked.

"You could say that," she replied, smiling.

I pushed myself up from the floor and touched my face with my fingertips. It felt foreign to me. Especially my cheekbones and nose. Then I looked down at my legs and noticed they were much shorter.

"This is so weird," I said, looking past Adrianne, toward Kendra, who was trying to stand. She looked exactly like the girl she'd selected from the magazine. Our eyes met and she gave me a weak smile.

"You can say that again. I look like a cheerleader," said Megan, staring at her reflection in a small mirror. Her hair was blonde, her skin tan, and when she smiled, I noticed she now had dimples.

"I'm actually surprised you chose that picture," said Kendra, who also had blonde hair but with light skin and freckles.

"I wanted to see how the other half lives, for once," she said, putting the mirror down. "I might regret it later but it will be fun playing an airhead."

"Just because you're a blonde doesn't make you an airhead," said Willow, frowning.

"Well, this one will be," she answered. "If I'm going to do this, I may as well have a little fun with it. Besides, I'm supposed to be from Sweden, right? Aren't they usually blonde and bubbleheads?"

"That's a stereotype and a very bad one. Anyway, acting 'dumb' doesn't sound like much fun to me," I said and glanced at Willow, who now looked like she was of Asian descent. "You look very pretty."

Willow smiled and ran her hand over her long, silky dark hair. "Thank you."

"You know, we are supposed to be sisters," said Megan, frowning at Willow. "I mean, I don't think we could look *any* different."

"We're supposed to be *step*-sisters. So, I can look any way I'd like," countered Willow, raising her chin.

"I should have gone Asian," said Megan, sighing. "I have a feeling I'm going to regret my choice anyway."

"Nonsense, you all look beautiful," said Clarice. "And now that you all have your new faces, we need to get moving. Although Marigold is helping us, she can be a bit frosty at times and won't like to be kept waiting."

I grabbed the mirror and looked over my appearance quickly. I was the splitting image of the model with the dark red hair and brown eyes. Satisfied, I put the mirror back down. "Okay. I'm ready when you are."

"What about our wands?" asked Kendra.

"Take them with you, but keep them hidden," said Adrianne.

"What will we do about getting new ones to use at the school?" I asked.

"Marigold is going to set you up with some," said Clarice.

'Okay," I replied.

We said our goodbyes to Adrianne, Opal, Rebecca, and Adele.

"Don't forget to call Bea," I reminded them. "I don't want to lose my job."

"Don't worry. I'm on it," said Clarice, holding up her cell phone.

"Thank you," I replied.

Bailey grabbed my hand. "You ready?"

"I'm ready for this to be over with," I said.

He nodded. "Yeah. I know. Don't worry, I'm going to help search for Vivian and make sure she doesn't get out of that globe."

"Thanks," I replied, thinking that if they didn't find her by the time the potion wore off, I'd leave the school myself and hunt her down. There was no way I wanted to go through that kind of ordeal again. I'd rather face Bella and Beldora.

Bailey, as if reading my thoughts, chuckled.

"What?" I asked.

"Nothing."

"*What*?" I insisted.

"I was just thinking that even with this disguise, I'd recognize you anywhere."

"Why is that?"

"Because you have this very determined look in your eyes all the time," he said. "At least lately."

"He means stubborn," said Kendra, overhearing us.

"You both do," said Adrianne. "Which is why I'm going to send you off with a very important warning. One that I don't want you to ignore."

"What?" I asked.

"Whatever happens, don't leave the school," she said. "Unless your life is in eminent danger."

"We won't. Speaking of leaving the school, what about our brooms?" I asked, wanting to get back into the sky again.

"Normally, I'd say bring it," said Adrianne. "But, Clarice recognized yours. I don't think it's a good idea to bring it."

I sighed. "Okay."

"What about the rest of us?" asked Kendra.

"I don't even have a broom," said Willow.

"I do," said Megan. "Only, I didn't bring it."

"That's fine. You won't be needing your brooms," said Adrianne. She looked at Clarice. "If they do, we'll figure it out later."

Clarice nodded.

"If you ask me, it's better this way. I wasn't kidding when I said that we don't want any of you leaving the school," said Adrianne, staring at us hard. "Knowing that you girls are safe is going to allow us to do what we need to do to get the globe and spell book back. I don't want to have to worry about where you're at."

"Don't worry," said Kendra. "We'll stay put."

She nodded and looked at her watch. "Good. Now, off with you. We don't want to keep the dean waiting any longer."

"No, we certainly don't," said Clarice. "Goodbye, Adrianne. I'll be back soon."

She nodded and stepped back.

"Wands raised," said Clarice. "To The Roix."

"To The Roix," the four of us repeated.

CHAPTER ELEVEN

Kala

The Roix was located in the Canadian Rocky Mountains, near Banff National Park. They'd built the school into the side of the mountain and Clarice explained that it only appeared to those who practiced magic. We teleported directly into Marigold Weiss's office, so I'd yet to see the outside of the school, but from looking through the pamphlet earlier, I knew it was the size of a small city.

"Thank goodness you're here. I was getting worried," said Dean Marigold, who was wearing a pink terrycloth robe and slippers. Somewhere in in her fifties, she had gray hair piled into a bun on her head, and large crystal eyes that reminded me of the late Hollywood actress, Bette Davis.

"Sorry we're late," said Clarice, walking toward Marigold, who was seated behind a large, cluttered desk. There were piles of paperwork and odd looking objects, which I had a feeling were mostly enchanted items. "We had an incident at Adrianne's. Bella and Beldora showed up."

Marigold's eyebrows shot up. "So, they *are* after the girls' wands?"

"Definitely," she replied. "But, Adrianne confronted and scared them off."

"They'll soon be back, so it's good that you left when you did. Speaking of – which one of you are Adrianne's daughters, Kendra and Kala?" asked Marigold, turning toward us.

"We are," said Kendra, raising her hand. "I'm Kendra and," she nodded toward me, "that's Kala. Those two are Willow and Megan."

Marigold nodded slowly. "And who might you be?" she asked, turning toward Tyler and Bailey.

"Boyfriend," they both said unanimously.

I smiled at Bailey.

He winked at me.

"Hmm... In case you didn't know, this is an *all* girl's school and we don't usually permit men on the premises," said Marigold, staring hard at them. "Obviously, you can't stay here."

"Understandable," said Bailey. "We were just making sure the girls arrived safely."

"Rest assured... they are all in good hands with me," she replied.

"That's what we're hoping," he replied, staring back at her evenly.

I couldn't help but smile at Bailey once again. He wasn't a pushover.

Marigold stared at him for another moment and then looked back to us. "Well then, it's late. Are you girls ready to see your rooms?"

We all nodded.

"Excellent." Marigold motioned toward Bailey and Tyler. "You boys had better say your goodbyes quickly. I also want to reiterate the fact that the girls are not allowed any male visitors. It's the same for all of our students."

"So, there are no male witches here either?" asked Kendra.

Marigold shook her head. "No. We are an 'all girls' school."

"Why is that?" I asked, frowning. From Marigold's expression, I had a feeling she didn't like men very much.

"It would be too distracting for both. You're here to learn and not to fraternize with the other sex," she answered.

Megan cleared her throat. "You're actually creating *more* distractions by doing that."

"Is that right? Would you care to explain?" asked Marigold with a disapproving look.

Megan looked at her like she was clueless. "Missing our boyfriends is a distraction."

The dean smirked. "I'm sorry, but that argument is a little weak. Besides, most girls at the school don't have boyfriends."

"How could they?" asked Megan. "And not only that, you're not allowing them to learn how to socialize with the opposite sex. That's important in today's society. I'm not just talking about flirting, either. I'm talking about having normal conversations."

"You're here to learn about magic. If you wish to spend time with boys, you may do so away from the premises and on the weekends," she said.

"Obviously, we can't," muttered Kendra, looking at Tyler.

"Okay. Enough." Clarice looked at the dean. "I'm sorry."

"It's fine," replied Marigold. "I don't mind talking about the school's rules. They're there for a reason and should be understood."

"I agree. Now," said Clarice, looking very cross. "Instead of questioning the rules of this school, I think you should all be grateful that Dean Weiss is taking you under her wing. She's doing this as a favor and I don't want her regretting it."

Megan sighed and apologized.

"Apology accepted. Just don't forget the rules about male visitors," said Marigold. "And we'll get along just fine."

Megan's eye twitched.

"You know, we do have a Debate Club," said Marigold. "Maybe you should join?"

"I doubt there is much to debate about if there aren't any boys in the club," said Megan dryly.

The dean smiled. "Touché."

I yawned.

"We'd better go," said Bailey, turning toward me. He pulled me into his arms and whispered in my ear. "Better stay on her good side."

"I have a feeling that won't be easy," I whispered back.

"Me too, but I hope we're wrong, If you run into any kind of trouble, though, you call me. I'll get here as quickly as possible," he said.

"I will," I replied, closing my eyes. This time, it actually felt good to have him worried about me.

Bailey pulled back and gave me a quick kiss on the lips. "Don't worry," he said afterward. "Like I said before, we'll find Vivian and that spell book. I won't rest until we do."

I nodded.

"Okay then," said Marigold, pushing the top button on her pen several times. "We'd better get you girls to your rooms."

"Thank you again for doing this," said Clarice. "Is there anything else you need from me?"

"No. I don't think so," replied Marigold. "I've enrolled the girls under their new identities and found them wands to use."

"Where did you get them?" I asked, curious.

"The Lost-and-Found."

"The Lost-and-Found? Won't someone else be missing them?" asked Kendra.

"As far as I'm concerned, if a witch isn't responsible enough to keep her wand in her possession, she doesn't deserve it," said Marigold. "So, make sure you keep your wands close at all times."

Clarice dug into her satchel and pulled out a checkbook. "How much do I owe you?"

"Don't worry, the school will bill you for the tuition," she replied. "After things have settled down, of course."

"Okay. What about the wands?" asked Clarice, shoving her checkbook back into her purse.

"Actually, you can just consider them gifts," she replied.

"I don't know what we'd have done without you, Marigold. I'm very grateful for everything. Thank you," repeated Clarice.

"You're welcome. Just keep me posted about Vivian. I can't imagine what will happen if those two bumbling idiots release her from the globe," she said.

"Nothing good, that's for sure," replied Clarice before turning to us. "As for you girls, I'll keep you posted as to what's happening."

"You'll call us later today?" I asked her.

"One of us will," she replied.

"Goodbye, Clarice," said Kendra, throwing her arms around her.

Clarice patted her on the back and whispered something. Kendra nodded and glanced at me. I gave her a questioning look, which she ignored.

"Goodbye, honey," Clarice said, walking over to me. She hugged me and whispered, "Remember what your mother said about Penelope. Keep that wand of yours hidden safely. Maybe in the floorboards underneath your bed?"

"Good idea," I whispered back.

She released me and then gave Willow and Megan a hug. Willow hugged her back, but Megan looked more uncomfortable than anything.

Some people just don't like to be hugged, said Vee.

I clenched my jaw. *And some people don't like having voices in their head.*

This time, Vee didn't respond.

Clarice nodded toward Bailey and Tyler. "Let's go, boys. They need to get some sleep and we have a lot to do."

Tyler gave Kendra a kiss and then moments later, it was just the four of us alone with Marigold.

"Now that your cousin is gone," she said, pulling out a ring of keys, "you'll need to think of me as your only confidante in this school. Do not share your true identities with anyone. *Anyone*. And... if they should become known, I want you to inform me immediately, so we can get you to safety. Understand?"

We all agreed.

"Now, later today, before I show you to your classes, we'll meet in my office again and we'll go over some things. It's important that you each stick to your stories, for obvious reasons. Do you have any questions?"

Nobody said anything.

"Good. Now, the moment we leave my office, you will no longer call each other by your real names. Understand?"

We all nodded.

Satisfied, she stood up. "Okay then. Let me show you to your rooms," she said and then headed toward the doorway.

"Are we going to each have our own room?" asked Megan.

She motioned toward Willow. "No. You and your 'sister' will share a room." Marigold looked at me and Kendra. "So will you two."

"So, we're not going to be divided into... sanctions?" asked Kendra.

"This isn't Hogwarts," said Marigold, looking amused. "However, since Kala has a dark wand in her possession, a couple of her classes will be slightly different than the rest of yours."

"But, my wand is to be hidden from sight," I replied. "So, what's the point?"

"The wand I'm loaning you is also one that can be used for Black magic," she explained.

"Really? And Clarice *agreed* to this?" I asked, surprised.

"She was the one who recommended it," said Marigold. "The wand isn't as powerful as yours, but you'll learn how to control it. You'll also learn how to use dark magic for the better good."

"I didn't know you could do that," said Megan, looking thoughtful. "Maybe I should start using a dark wand."

"You'll need to discuss that with your mother. When it comes to magic, I'm quite sure that there are a lot of things that you girls don't know yet. But, if you stay here long enough, that will change. *You* will change," she said. "So, you should really look at this as an opportunity to improve your magical skills and not just a place to hide."

"That's how I'm trying to look at it," said Willow, who'd been mostly quiet. "I mean, we need all the help we can get, right?"

Marigold nodded. "Exactly, and one can never learn too much about magic. Now, don't forget your luggage."

We picked up our bags and Marigold led us out of her office and into a wide, dimly lit corridor. From there, she led us down several hallways until we reached a spiral staircase.

"What floor are our rooms on?" asked Willow, staring up at the winding stairway.

"Just up a couple of flights to the west wing," said Marigold, who began climbing up. "By the way, I don't know if Clarice told you but the school is haunted."

"No, she didn't," said Megan, stiffening up.

"Yes. They're just poltergeists but the little rascals love to cause trouble. So, if you notice anything unusual, just do your best to ignore it. They thrive on attention and once you acknowledge them, the pests will never leave you alone," said Marigold.

"What do you mean by *unusual*?" asked Willow.

Before Marigold could answer, a large red ball appeared out of nowhere, hovering in thin air at the top of the stairs. It dropped down onto the wooden step and began to bounce toward us.

"Ignore it," reminded Marigold, under her breath.

We all stepped to the side as it descended past us.

"You… you said they're harmless, right?" asked Megan.

"Only if you ignore them. Otherwise, their pranks will escalate, which can sometimes be rather troublesome," said Marigold, climbing up the steps again.

"Great," said Megan. "This place just keeps getting better and better."

"Are you okay?" I asked, noticing how troubled she looked.

"I just really hate ghosts," she mumbled, her eyes darting around. "They freak the heck out of me."

Marigold, who was starting to become a little breathless, looked back at us over her shoulder. "You'd... be wise to keep that to yourself. Hopefully... none of them... heard."

There was a loud screech and then a large white face with black eyes, and a horrific smile appeared next to Megan. She screamed and pulled me in front of her. Laughing evilly, the ghoulish face disappeared.

"Great. Now you've done it," said Marigold, shaking her head in dismay. "Well, don't say that I didn't warn you."

"Can't you control them?" I asked, my heart pounding in my chest. I'd never seen a poltergeist or any kind of ghost before and even I had to admit that it was unnerving.

"No. Unfortunately, we have no power over the dead," said the dean.

"What about performing some kind of an exorcism?" Megan asked.

"That would involve bringing in the church and outsiders," said Marigold. "We obviously can't do that."

"All I can say is that they'd better leave me alone or I'm freaken out of here," mumbled Megan.

I thought about the spell book I'd taken home with me, the night before. I'd read something about spirits. "I read somewhere that you could control them with Black magic."

"Technically, yes. If one were to call upon a demon to take care of the spirits. But that's not something we condone. Face it, girls, you're just going to have to live with them," said Marigold, reaching the second floor.

"Can we at least keep them out of our bedrooms?" asked Megan.

"Fortunately, that we can do," said Marigold. "I know of a couple of different spells that will prohibit them from entering your room. We'll do that right away, so you don't have to worry about the pesky rascals."

"I'd appreciate that," answered Megan, relieved. "I don't see why you wouldn't do that anyway. I can't imagine any of the other students wanting uninvited visitors sneaking up on them in their rooms."

"Honestly, the poltergeists usually just haunt the main atrium and the cafeteria. As I said, they thrive on attention and often try their little pranks in front of an audience. You're fresh meat, though. I'm sure that's why they're being rambunctious at the moment," said Marigold.

I stared past her at a painting of one of the late presidents. As I was turning away, a white face appeared in front of the picture. It smiled and worms began crawling out of its rancid mouth. Shuddering, I ignored the ghoul and kept walking.

"So, where are our rooms?" asked Kendra, her eyes wide. I looked to where she was staring and noticed the same wormy face I'd seen trying to freak her out.

Marigold pointed down a hallway to the left. "Just down this way."

We followed her quietly, past several doorways, until we reached the end of the hallway. Standing between two doors, she began unlocking one of them.

"You two will be in this one. Number two-fourteen," she said, nodding toward me and Kendra.

"What about us?" asked Megan.

"You're just across the hall," said Marigold, turning to unlock the other door, "two-thirteen."

I pushed the door open to our room and flicked on the light. I wasn't sure what I'd expected, but the room was very plain and not very homey. There were two twin beds, a large brown dresser, and two matching nightstands, one for each of us.

"What do you think?" asked Marigold, peeking her head through the doorway.

"It's… fine," I said, looking around the room. I noticed that here was another door in the back of the bedroom and a small closet.

Marigold nodded toward the beds. Each came with a solid gray blanket and white pillow. "Just so you know, you can decorate it any way you'd like. It's why we keep the rooms simple."

I smiled. "Oh. Okay."

Marigold glanced around the room again. "Do either of you know any interior design spells?"

"Not yet," said Kendra, setting her traveling bag onto one of the beds.

"No worries. You'll learn some here at the school," she replied and then nodded toward the alarm clock. "Now, meet me back in my office at six thirty a.m. *sharp.* I'll go over your classes and then introduce you to your first teacher."

Kendra and I both looked at the clock.

I cringed.

We only had about three hours to sleep and I knew she wasn't a morning person.

"Believe me, I know you're going to be tired. So will I. But, classes begin at seven and even magic won't change that," said Marigold, noticing our dour expressions. "So, just try and get as much sleep as you can."

"It's okay," said Kendra, forcing a smile onto her face. "We're very grateful for your help and wouldn't dream of creating any problems for you. We'll be there right at six-thirty. Right, Kala?"

I nodded.

"Don't forget. Use your new names," reminded Marigold.

She blushed. "Yes. Sorry."

"Don't worry. We'll be there," I said, sitting down on the other bed. "Both Cousin *Jane* and I."

"Good," said the dean, smiling in approval. "Now, get some sleep. You have a big day ahead of you."

"We will. Goodnight," said Kendra.

"Goodnight," said Marigold.

"Wait," I said, as she was about to close the door. "What about the protection spell? To keep the ghosts out?"

"Oh. Right." Marigold raised her wand and chanted something that I couldn't quite hear. There was a flash of light and then the room smelled like some kind of herb.

"What's that smell?" asked Kendra, wrinkling her nose.

"It's sage and fennel," said Marigold, slipping her wand back into the pocket of her robe. "Wards off evil spirits and negativity."

"Thanks, Marigold," I said.

"From here on out, you'll need to call me Dean Weiss or Ms. Weiss," she said. "Anything else wouldn't be appropriate."

"Sure," I replied, unzipping my luggage bag. "Goodnight, Dean Weiss."

"Goodnight," she said and then slipped out.

I turned to look at my sister. "So, what do you think?" I asked softly.

"I think if we have to stay here longer than a week, I'm going to go freaken crazy."

I couldn't have agreed more.

CHAPTER TWELVE

Kala

Just as Clarice suggested, we found hiding spots for our wands under the floorboards. After pulling up a panel in the walk-in closet, we wrapped up Penelope and Chloe in hand towels, and hid them together.

"Do you think they'll be okay like this? Together?" asked Kendra as we walked out of the closet.

I shrugged. "I've never hidden a wand before, let alone two. I would think they'd be fine, since they're kind of like us. Sisters."

"Maybe. They do bicker sometimes, though. For all we know, they're arguing right now."

I snickered. "Yeah, very true. I'm sure they'll be fine, though. At least we wrapped them separately. That should help."

Kendra chewed on her lower lip. "Maybe we should ask them if they mind being so close?"

"No. That would be letting the wands control *us*, right?" I said. "We can't do that."

She smiled. "True. You're starting to sound like Mom and Clarice."

"How can I not... when all they do is lecture me about Penelope. Anyway, speaking of wands... I wonder when we're getting the new ones?"

"Hopefully, when we see Marigold later. I already feel lost without Chloe, though. This really sucks."

"Yeah. Now you know how I've been feeling. Everyone wants me to get rid of Penelope. She seems almost part of me now, though. I don't want to let her go."

"As long as you're not doing anything bad with her, I can't see why you should have to get rid of the wand," she replied.

I snorted. "I would never do anything bad. You know me," I said, meaning it.

"At least you'd never do anything intentionally," she replied and then sighed. "Look, we haven't been spending a lot of time together lately, which I never thought would bother me, but it does. I know it's partly my fault. I've been with Tyler and working..."

"Don't be so hard on yourself. I've been really busy too. With my new job and Bailey. So, it's not just your fault."

She smiled. "I guess we'll be spending a lot more time together here though, huh?"

"Yes," I said. "Although, you look like a stranger."

"So do you," she said, laughing. "It's even weirder looking down at you. What are you, five feet?"

"If I'm lucky," I replied, the both of us standing in front of the mirror.

"It's cute. If you get bullied, though, let me know." She slid her arm over my shoulder and placed the side of her head against mine. "For any reason. We have to stick together."

I smiled at her in the mirror. "We will. No matter what."

I knew Kendra and I didn't always see eye-to-eye, and there were times that we could go weeks without talking to each other, but... there was no doubt in my mind that we'd risk our lives to save one another. Our relationship was so much different than Adrianne and her sister's. I couldn't imagine trying to kill my sister. The thought made me sick to my stomach.

She yawned and dropped her arm. "We'd better get some sleep. I'm going to be grumpy enough as it is. "

"That goes for both of us," I said.

We both took turns in the shower and then fell fast asleep. It seemed as if I'd just closed my eyes when a whistling noise startled me out of a dead sleep. Opening my eyes, I looked over at Kendra and found her sleeping. Sighing, I closed my eyes and began drifting back to sleep.

"Rise and shine, girls! Up and at 'em!"

Gasping, I opened my eyes back up and stared in shock at what was standing on the nightstand, separating our beds. It appeared to be a small, female elf. Her long, brown hair was pulled into a ponytail and she was clothed in shorts and a blue T-shirt with the school's logo on it.

She let go of the whistle hanging from her neck, and smiled. "Hello! Are you ready for a super-exciting first day of school? I know that we're all so excited to have you here," she said with bubbly enthusiasm.

"I... who are you?"

"The name is Candace."

Admittedly, she was cute with her beautiful iridescent wings, large violet eyes, and pointy ears which were pierced with a rainbow of gem earrings. But, I was tired and ornery. "Candace, I'm not sure what you're doing in our room, but we have at least another thirty minutes to sleep. So, please... go away."

The elf looked at the watch on her wrist. "No can do. Sorry. You have sixty minutes to get dressed, eat a hearty breakfast, and do a round of cardio," she said in a sing-song voice.

"A round of cardio?" I repeated.

"Yes. It's going to wake you both up and make your day that much brighter." She began to cheer. "Cardio, cardio, makes us smart! Cardio, cardio, is good for the heart!"

I groaned.

"Now, who's with me?" hollered Candace.

Her enthusiastic zippiness was making my head spin. Not that I didn't appreciate her peppy attitude. It was just too early. "Why don't you start without us and we'll catch up in a little while," I said, pulling the blanket over my head.

She blew the whistle again. "Sorry, but rules are rules and I have a job to do. You need to get up so we can get your cardio on!"

"Tell me this is a dream," said Kendra hoarsely from the other bed. "Please."

"It's a dream," I mumbled.

"Is this a dream?" asked the elf. She moved closer to me and I let out a squeal when she pinched my ear.

I gasped. "Stop it!"

"I'll stop when you get up," she answered, this time pulling a piece of my hair.

"Ouch! Good grief, make it go away," I moaned.

"I am not an 'it'. Now, come on, you two lazy bones...," whined the frustrated elf. "You *both* have to get up. We don't have all day."

"Who are you, exactly?" asked Kendra, sitting up. "Our personal trainer?"

I gave the elf a stern look. "I sure hope not."

"What I am is *yours* for the duration of time you spend here at the school," said the elf, now looking at some kind of miniature clipboard. "For your information, my official *title* is Room Advisor. I'm responsible for getting you to where you need to get to in the morning. This also includes making sure you've had breakfast and a little exercise."

"For one, I *don't* exercise. At least not before noon," said Kendra. "For two, I'm not hungry. I seriously doubt Kala is either."

My eyes widened at Kendra's use of my name. Noticing her mistake, she cringed. Fortunately, the elf didn't seem to notice.

"This isn't the Four Seasons," she said, tapping her pen against the clipboard. "And rules are rules. Get dressed and I'll meet you in the hallway in fifteen minutes."

"Fine," I huffed. "Just let us get dressed."

She stared at me. "Okay. Just don't make me come back in here and get the two of you."

"We won't," we both mumbled at the same time.

Smiling again, the elf leaped off of the nightstand and began running toward the door.

"What did you say your name was?" asked Kendra.

"It's Candy," I said.

The elf turned and gave me a dirty look. "Call me Candy and see where that gets you."

"Sorry," I said, more amused than anything.

"It's okay," she said, relaxing. "You didn't know. I just hate that name. I used to get teased when I was younger."

"Gotcha," said Kendra. "I was teased in school, so I can respect that."

"Me too," I said. "Um, I wasn't teased but I can respect that."

"Thank you. Now, get dressed and I'll meet you in the hallway."

"Morning workouts," mumbled Kendra, when Candace magically disappeared through the doorway. "We are definitely getting out of here as soon as possible."

"Too bad it won't be before cardio," I said, flinging the blanket away from me.

CHAPTER THIRTEEN

Kala

We grudgingly got through the exercise session with Candace, after having oat bran muffins and orange juice. Afterward, we ran into Willow and Megan on the way to Marigold's. From the look on their faces, I knew they'd been through the same thing that we had.

"So, how was your morning?" asked Kendra with a small smile.

Megan grunted. "Don't even get me started."

"Let me guess. You met your Room Adviser?" I asked.

"You mean the Elf on the Shelf's evil twin?" asked Megan. "Sherry the Shrew, is what we've dubbed the little monster. Can you believe it – she actually threw a cup of water at me when I refused to get out of bed."

Kendra and I both smiled.

"It took everything that I had not to turn her into a mouse and flush her down the toilet. Seriously, I was *not* happy. And then to force us to work *out?* I mean, I thought this was a school of magic. Not a fitness club," said Megan, wiping a sheen of sweat from her forehead.

"I know. Ours had us doing relay races and squats," I replied, knowing that I was going to be sore tomorrow. "Marigold should have warned us."

"Yeah. It would have been nice to know these things. Still, I have to admit, I feel pretty good after that short aerobic workout," said Willow.

"How could you feel good?" asked Megan. "We only had about two hours of sleep."

Willow shrugged. "I have no idea. But, I actually have more energy than before."

"Not me. I feel like I could sleep for a week," said Megan.

I leaned closer to Willow and asked if she hidden her wand.

"Yes. It was hard, though. I have never gone anywhere without Juniper. I feel like I'm missing my right arm," she said, looking unhappy.

"I know what you mean. I'm really not comfortable knowing that we can't carry them," said Kendra as we stopped outside of Marigold's office.

"It seems like it's almost more dangerous not having the wands in our possession," said Willow. "I don't know why we can't just hide them without using them."

"I know. I don't get it," said Kendra, knocking on the dean's door.

"Come in," called Marigold.

We opened the door and walked into her office.

"There you are," said Marigold, smiling brightly at us from behind her desk. "How is everyone doing this morning?"

"Not very good," said Megan, frowning. "Especially after that early morning cardio workout. Why didn't you forewarn us about the elves?"

Marigold's smile fell. "Goodness, I'm so sorry about that. It completely slipped my mind. It's a new program that the Holistic Health Department is testing out. With all of these new-aged electronic gadgets, they claim that our witches are in need of more exercise and healthier eating."

"So, we should expect this every morning?" asked Megan, less than thrilled.

"Afraid so," said Marigold. "Just remember to go to bed at a reasonable hour and eventually, you'll begin to look forward to the new routine."

"Yeah, I really hate doing Gym class at my current school. I can't imagine why I'd feel any better about it here."

"I don't mind," said Willow. "I've never worked out with an instructor before. I found it rather fun."

Megan rolled her eyes. "Fun? You really need to get out more."

"Nonsense. She has a very positive attitude. That's what I like to see," said Marigold, reaching into a drawer under her desk. She pulled out four velvet bags and then shoved a pair of small, blue reading glasses onto the bridge of her nose. "Now, our time is running out. Here are your new wands. Oh, and Megan, you're also getting a new one. Since the wand you currently use has been handed down from generation to generation, your mother thought it was best to use something without your family crest on it. Just in case. We don't want any of you linked back to Bayport."

"Sweet," said Megan, smiling for the first time. "Can I take it home with me?"

"Yes, as long as you don't lose them, of course," Marigold said, handing us each a bag. "Obviously, these aren't 'bonding' wands, as those are very, very rare, but believe me, these lovelies are all quite powerful in their own right. So, be careful when handling them."

"Do they talk?" I asked, pulling my wand out of the bag. It was the color of dark mahogany and slightly bent, just before the tip.

"They can *all* talk," said Marigold, looking at me over her glasses. "It's more of a matter of, *will* they?"

"Sometimes it's better if they just keep quiet," said Kendra in a low voice. "I mean, Penelope isn't exactly the friendliest of wands. Right, Kala?"

"She has her moments, that's for sure. So, this wand is really for practicing Black magic?" I asked, studying it.

"Yes. Yours actually has the power to perform both. Which is why you must be extremely careful with it," she replied. "And for goodness sake, don't lose it like the last girl did."

"Do you know who owned it before me?" I asked, curious.

"Yes, as a matter of fact I do," replied Marigold. "Of course, I am not allowed to divulge who she is; I can only say that she's no longer at this school."

"Why? Because she lost her wand?" asked Willow.

She licked her lips and it took a while for her to answer. "There were many reasons why that particular student was expelled. That's all that I can say. Just don't lose your wands and please... be good, girls."

"You don't have to worry about us," said Kendra. "We'll stay out of trouble."

"I figured you would. Clarice said some very nice things about you. It's such a pity that you've had to deal with such awful things. Hopefully, your time here will help take your mind off of Vivian and the pain she's put you all through."

"I'm just excited to learn more about magic and spells," said Willow.

"That's right. You have never been to any kind of school before, have you, dear?" asked Marigold.

"Not since I was really young. I've had to learn almost everything on my own," she replied matter-of-factly.

"You do know how to read?" asked Marigold.

"Yes and I know how to write along with some basic math," said Willow.

"If you're up for it, I'm going to have you take some additional classes in the evenings. To get you caught up in the skills you'll need to get your GED," said Marigold. "You do want your GED, correct?"

"What is that?" asked Willow.

The dean explained that it was what some people acquired if, for some reason, they hadn't earned enough school credits to receive a high school diploma.

"Since you're nineteen, I would recommend going that route. You'll need a diploma or a GED to get into college anyway," she said.

"Yes. I would definitely be interested in doing that," said Willow, brightening. "I really could go to college?"

"Yes, you certainly could," said Marigold. "And should."

"Perfect. Sign me up," said Willow.

"Very good. I'll get you enrolled in that, too," replied Marigold, writing herself a note.

"Sorry to change the subject, but are the rest of our wands just for White magic?" asked Kendra, turning hers over in her hand and studying it. It was made of birch and there was a white flower painted near the handle.

"Yes," answered the dean, setting her pen down. "Why?"

"Just curious," she answered.

"My goodness, the time is just flying by," said Marigold, glancing at the clock. She got up and walked over to the other side of the room and picked up four garment bags. "I have your robes."

"Excuse me, but what kind of a flower is this?" asked Kendra, nodding toward her wand.

"It's a tuberose," said Marigold, walking back toward us. "It symbolizes purity of the mind."

Megan snorted. "Guess you'd better keep Tyler out of your head when your casting spells. You might break the wand with some of your wicked thoughts."

Kendra's cheeks turned pink. "Speak for yourself. I have no wicked thoughts about Tyler."

"Liar," said Megan, smirking.

"Whatever," replied Kendra, looking like she wanted to hit Megan with her wand.

"Does that embarrass you?" asked Megan, amused.

A vein in Kendra's forehead began to throb. "No. Can we just drop the subject?"

"What's the big deal?" asked Megan.

"Leave her alone," I said sharply.

"Relax. I'm not judging her," said Megan. "I doubt any of us are pure of mind. Even you, Kala. Especially with such a hot boyfriend like Bailey. What's it like kissing a shifter?"

"That's none of your business," I replied, noticing out of the corner of my eye that the dean was growing angry.

"Enough of this. We have more important matters to discuss and boys are definitely not on the list," said the dean in a tight voice. She began handing out garment bags. "Now, here's an official school robe for each of you. Your 'names' have been embroidered onto the fabric."

"What do we wear underneath?" asked Megan.

"Anything you'd like," said the dean. "Most girls are comfortable in shorts and a T-shirt, but it's up to you."

"Speaking of clothes," I replied, opening up the bag. "Will we have time to shower and change before our first class? I feel a little gross after the workout."

"Don't worry. I'll show you how to do a Refresh spell in just a second," said Marigold, sitting back down. "First, I would like to hand you your class schedules." She grabbed a small stack of papers sitting on her desk and handed each of us one. "You'll notice that there are a couple of classes you'll take together, like Potions, Enchanted Objects, and Herbal Medicine. Kala will also join you in Spell Casting, but she'll have an extra class, at the end of the day. The Ins and Outs of Dark Arts. It will teach you how to use your wand responsibly."

"Can I take that class, too? I'd like to learn something about Black magic," said Megan.

"Why?" asked Kendra. "Your wand is for White."

"I just think it would be an interesting subject. Besides, 'know your enemy', right? Obviously, the information would be useful in protecting ourselves."

"I couldn't agree more," said Marigold. "And you'll learn all of that in the other classes. This one is strictly for those who own a Black magic wand. If you really want a different wand, you'll need to take that up with your mother."

"Fine," mumbled Megan, sitting back in her seat.

"Now, you all have your stories straight?" asked Marigold a few seconds later.

"Yes," we all replied in unison.

"Good. As I stated before, if you do run into some kind of trouble, find me and we'll get things sorted out," said Marigold.

There was a sudden knock on the door.

Marigold frowned and called out, "Yes?"

The door opened and a woman with short dark hair and heavy makeup peeked her head through it. "Sorry to interrupt. There is another new enrollee waiting for you in the hallway."

Marigold's eyes widened. "Another new student? Goodness, this is a busy week."

"Yes. The word must be spreading about what a magnificent school you're running," said the other woman, glancing our way. She smiled. "Welcome, ladies. My name is Ms. Hotchkins. I'm sure I'll be seeing all of you in my Potions class."

We smiled and said, "Hello."

"Tell the other student that I'll be with her in a minute, please Sybil?" requested the dean.

"I will certainly do that," replied the woman before closing the door.

"Okay, it's time to change into your school robes so you can be on your way to class," said Marigold. "We'd better hurry."

"Wait. You mentioned something about a Refresh spell?" I said, knowing that my armpits really needed it.

"Oh. Yes. I almost forgot. All you have to do is hold your wand above your head and say the words "Refresh, clean, and press." Not only will you feel like you've recently showered, but your clothing will also smell like it was just laundered."

It reminded me of the spell our mother Adrianne had placed on us, before sneaking into Vivian's coven. Thinking of her warm, reassuring smile, I missed her already. Especially knowing that we couldn't see her for who knew how long.

"Go ahead. Give it a whirl," prodded Marigold, waving her hands at us. "We need to get moving."

I stood up and did what she'd instructed. A fresh smelling mist surrounded me and when it dissipated, I felt clean, and somehow dry, from head to toe. And sure enough, my clothing felt and smelled like I'd just taken it out of the dryer.

"That's so cool," said Willow, raising her wand and repeating the spell. I watched as the others did the same and soon, we were wearing our new robes and ready to leave for class.

"Since I have another new student to interview, I'm going to have Candace show you around the school before introducing you to Ms. Benky. She teaches Enchanted Objects, which you will all have for first period."

"Our Room Advisor?" I asked.

"Yes," said the dean. She cleared her throat and called out for the elf, who magically appeared next to us. "Candace, could you be so kind as to give the girls a tour of the school and then show them to their first class?"

"Of course, Dean Weiss," said the elf, who had changed into a cute little blue jumpsuit with matching heels. Her hair was now in a long braid down her back, and she had on sparkly eye makeup.

"You look so cute," said Willow, bending down to look at her. "I love your outfit."

Candace smiled and looked down. "Thank you. I made it."

"You're very talented," said Willow.

The elf blushed. "You're very kind."

"Why can't she be our Room Advisor?" asked Megan, waving her thumb at Candace. "Ours is cranky, bossy, and looks like a wrestler."

Marigold bit back a smile. "Now, now. Sherry is good at what she does. Besides, something tells me that you need a little extra push in the mornings."

"You sound like my mother," muttered Megan.

"And *she* sounds like a wise woman," said the dean. "Now, off you go, my young sorceresses. Classes will be starting very soon."

"Wait. If you hear anything from our family, about Vivian, could you please send us a message?" asked Willow.

"Of course," said Marigold, accompanying us to the doorway. "In all honesty, I'm just as curious as you are to find out what is happening. Hopefully, they'll sort things out very quickly."

"Let's hope," said Megan.

Candace moved in front of us. "Follow me, girls. I'll try and make this quick so you can get to your class quickly."

"Thank you, Candace," said Marigold.

As we walked out, I noticed Ms. Hotchkins standing in the corridor with the other student, a slender girl with a brown bob and sparkling green eyes.

"Hello," said the teenager, taking a step toward us. "I'm Dorie. You're new here, too?"

"Yes," said Kendra, staring at her curiously. "We are."

"Cool. I hate being the only new person at school. It's so awkward. Maybe we can do lunch together?" said Dorie.

"Maybe," said Megan. "I mean, we can try and save you a seat, but we've never been to the lunchroom before. So, don't take it personal if we can't find you."

"I won't and… thanks," said Dorie.

"You'd better get going, girls. Time is of the essence," said Marigold, shooing us away.

"That Dorie looks awfully familiar," said Willow, as we followed Candace away from the office.

"You think so?" I asked.

"Yes. I wonder if she's from Salem?" said Willow.

"You can ask her at lunch. That is if we all get through the first couple of hours of this place," grumbled Megan.

I looked back over my shoulder and noticed Ms. Hotchkins still standing in the hallway, studying us as we walked away. When she noticed me looking at her, she smiled and then turned the other direction, walking away quickly. I wasn't sure why, but something about the way she was watching us made me uneasy.

She suspects something about you and the others, said Vee.

Suspects what?

The voice didn't respond.

I'm going crazy, I thought, and then waited for the voice to disagree. The voice remained silent.

CHAPTER FOURTEEN

Beldora

"So, it says here... you are from Wisconsin, Dorie," said Dean Weiss, looking at the paperwork that Bella and Beldora had conjured up. "And that your father was a farmer and your mother a sorceress?"

"Yes. In fact, I just learned recently about my mother being a witch. You see, she and my father were recently killed in a car accident."

"I'm so sorry for your loss," said Marigold quickly, her eyes softening. "I didn't know."

Beldora smiled sadly. "Thank you. It's been very difficult. I actually had no idea of her background, but I did learn why she kept it from me."

"About her being a witch?"

"Yes. I found some old letters in her storage trunk, up in the attic. Along with a wand and her journal. She kept it from me and my father."

"If you don't want to share this information, I would totally understand," said the dean, who was leaning forward and listening intently.

But you want to know.... Beldora thought, smiling inwardly. From what Bella had learned, the dean lived for gossip. She was also very gullible, much like Sybil, who had believed the story as well.

"In her diaries she said that he would have never accepted her for what she really was and that she didn't want to take the chance of losing my father."

"So, all of these years, she lived a lie for him?" said Marigold, looking disgusted. "That's a shame."

So, she doesn't like men, thought Beldora, amused. "Yes. I wish she would have told me the truth when she was alive, though. I certainly wouldn't have judged her. In fact, I'm thrilled about it. It's why I wanted to enroll in this school. To learn as much as I can about being a witch. I feel as if it's my birthright, you know?"

"I would have to agree."

Beldora forced tears to her eyes. "I just wish that she would have shared this knowledge with me when she was alive." She began to cry. "I miss her so much. I feel so lost and alone."

"Do you have any other family?"

"Just my aunt," she replied, hoping that the old witch wouldn't ask about her. "We hardly know each other and she's barely making ends meet, from what I hear."

"That's too bad," said Marigold. "So, you're basically on your own now."

"Yes. The worst thing is that the banks are seizing my parents' farm and I don't know where I'm going to live."

Marigold grabbed a couple of tissues from her desk and held them out toward Beldora. "You poor thing," she said, her heart going out toward the grief-stricken girl. "Rest assured, you have found a new home here at The Roix."

"How will I pay for the enrollment?" she asked. "Like I said, I have no money."

"Don't worry about that right now. We'll figure something out. Maybe you can even get a job on campus," said the dean.

"Thank you," said Beldora, wiping her eyes and blowing her nose. "You're... so... so kind."

Marigold pushed her eyeglasses up and began typing on her laptop. "Let me approve your admission here quickly, and then we'll get you enrolled in some classes. Tell me, did you bring your mother's wand?"

Beldora pulled out her own wand and waved it around, like she wasn't sure what to do with it. "Yes. Here it is. I don't really know how to use it."

Marigold stared at her wide-eyed. "First of all, be careful and don't point it at anyone."

"Oh. Sorry," said Beldora, setting it down. "I had no idea."

Marigold took out her wand and waved it over Beldora's. "No harm done."

"What are you doing?" she asked.

"I'm testing it to find out what kind of magic it prefers to manifest."

"It's Black magic," said Beldora.

Marigold stop waving her wand. "How do you know?"

She gave her a weak smile. "I read about it in my mother's journals. Another reason she kept it from my father. He was a bible thumper."

Marigold frowned. "Bible thumper?"

"Yes. You know, someone who is always quoting stuff from the bible and is heavily into the church."

"I know what you meant. I'm just a little surprised that you used such a derogatory term to describe your father and his beliefs. Here at the school, you'll find that no matter what a person's spiritual beliefs are, we must never ridicule."

"I didn't mean to offend," said Beldora quickly.

"You didn't offend me but you might someone else. There is a melting pot of different cultures here at the school. Many different beliefs. Although we encourage freedom of speech, we also encourage respect for one another."

"I understand, and again, I'm sorry. My mother used to call him that and I just thought it was funny. I realize now that I was wrong. It wasn't funny."

"Whether it's wrong or right, just remember our policy and you'll get along well with the other students. I must say that I'm a little surprised that your mother and father stayed together if their beliefs were so different," said the dean, leaning back in her chair.

"You know what they say – you can't choose who you love, right?" laughed Beldora nervously.

"No. I guess not."

Marigold waved her wand over Beldora's once again, until a black aura surrounded it. "It appears that you were right," said the dean, putting her wand away.

"I told you," said Beldora innocently.

"So you did." Marigold turned and began typing into the computer. "You'll have to be careful with it. I'll need to enroll you in 'The Ins and Outs of Dark Arts'."

Beldora moved to the edge of her seat. Although she'd had this particular wand for almost two decades, she was always open to learning anything new that might help take down Semora, the self-righteous twit. "That sounds interesting. Will I get to learn some Black magical spells?"

"At this school, you will indeed learn spells but not Black ones," said the dean. "They are usually created for malevolent purposes and that's not we're about here at The Roix. We want to teach our students how to use magic in ways that will be better for our families, our friends, and of course, the community."

How quaint, thought Beldora. *I guess I won't be learning anything useful here.* "I understand."

"Good. Now, after we are finished signing you up, I'll show you to your room. Did you bring any luggage?"

"Uh, no. As a matter of fact, I wasn't sure if I would be staying here or not. I left it back in Wisconsin. At a motel."

"A motel? No worries. We can send one of our elves to retrieve your things while you're getting acclimated with the school."

"Actually, it's being taken care of," said Beldora. "Sybil volunteered."

"Sybil did? How nice of her." Marigold smiled.

The truth was that Sybil hadn't volunteered to do anything because she thought that 'Dorie' had been living with Bella. The lies were stacking up, but she wasn't planning on staying at the school for very long.

"Now that we've got that settled, I'll find you a robe and we'll get a move on. I'm sure you're excited to begin?"

"You have no idea," said Beldora.

CHAPTER FIFTEEN

Kala

Candace gave us a tour of the school, just as promised. Most of the hallways were quiet because most of the classes had already started

"How many witches belong to this school?" I asked.

"One-hundred and fifty-four, including you and the other girl, Dorie," said Candace.

"That's not very many," said Megan, looking surprised. "From the size of this place, I thought you were going to say five hundred."

"Oh no. The Roix is relatively new yet," said the elf. "And not everyone is admitted into the school. You were lucky you made the cut."

I wondered if we would have made it without the help of Clarice.

"It looks like some of our classes are *not* magic related, either," said Kendra, studying her agenda. Her face fell. "I even have Calculus, English Literature, and History."

"Yes," said Candace. "Even though this is a school of magic, you still need to earn the same amount of credits to get your diploma. I'm sure Dean Weiss was able to get a hold of your current school records to find out what credits you'll actually need to graduate."

"No wonder there are nine classes listed. It's going to be a long day," said Megan.

"But, it will go by quickly. The teachers make the classes enjoyable and… you'll learn so much. I can't wait to see how your first day goes," said Candace. "You'll have to tell me all about it."

"Don't worry. We'll tell you tomorrow morning, when you're torturing us again with exercise and bran muffins," I said and then winked.

"Hey, if you want to trade House Elves, just say it," said Megan. "We'll gladly take Candy and you can have Sherry."

"No way. And it's Candace. *Not* Candy," said Kendra.

The elf smiled. "For that, I'll go easy on your calisthenics tomorrow."

"Thanks," said Kendra.

When Candace was out of earshot, Megan leaned toward me and whispered, "Next time we do that doppelganger thing, I'm stealing Kendra's photo."

"Hopefully we won't be here long enough for that to happen," I replied.

"Let's hope," she said.

***

After showing us the lunchroom, media center, gymnasium, and courtyard, Candace brought us to our first class, Enchanted Objects. The classroom was large and looked like any other school room, but with only fifteen students and all of them dressed in the same blue robes. It was definitely odd and I knew it would take time to get used to. Had I not known we were witches, I would have thought it was some kind of weird cult.

This is a cult, said Vee. *A cult full of witches.*

"Oh, so you're back," I said out loud.

Kendra looked at me.

My cheeks turned pink. "Uh, sorry."

"Good Morning," said the teacher, a woman in her thirties. She had blonde hair pulled up into a bun and glasses. "I'm Ms. Benky. Welcome to my classroom."

We all thanked her.

"Why don't you girls take a seat?" she said, after introducing us to the class. "We have something very special going on today. I think you're all going to enjoy it."

The four of us found spots in the back of the room.

"By the way, thank you for bringing them here, Candace," said the teacher. "Would you like to sit in on our discussion? We've been talking about the enchanted stones of Fae Valley."

Candace's face lit up. "My village neighbors, the Fae. Of course I'd love to listen in."

"Where's Fae Valley?" asked Megan out loud.

"It's a secret place near the Northern Shores of Minnesota," said the elf, climbing up onto a vacant desk. She sat down on the table and crossed her legs. "It's a beautiful, magical place. I wish you could all see it."

"So, I've heard," said the teacher. "It is my understanding that mortals have never stepped foot inside of the valley, because it's protected by magic. Isn't that correct?"

"Yes," said Candace. "No humans have ever seen Fae Valley."

The teacher held up a small leather bag, a radiant smile on her face. "Which is why these enchanted stones are so precious." She opened up the bag and held up five separate stones for us to see and then placed them on her desk, in the front of the classroom. As far as I could tell, the white stones looked like simple agates. At least from where I was sitting.

"These rare stones were donated by the gracious Fairy council of Fae Valley," said Ms. Benky.

"What do they do?" asked a girl with long red hair and glasses, seated in the front row.

Candace, who must have known, giggled and then covered her mouth.

"That, my dear Emily, is what you are all going to find out. Now, who would like to come up to the front and help me demonstrate?"

Almost everyone in the classroom held up their hand, including Willow.

"How about you, Sara?"

Nobody said anything.

Kendra cleared her throat loudly.

"Don't be shy," said the teacher, who I now realized was looking directly at me. "This is a great opportunity to get your feet wet right away in my class."

My cheeks turned red. I'd forgotten my 'name' already. "Uh, sure. Why not?"

Ms. Benky smiled.

I stood up and walked over to her desk, feeling all eyes upon me.

"Hold out your hand," said Ms. Benky.

I did what she asked and the teacher dropped a stone into my palm. I rubbed my thumb over it, expecting to feel some kind of vibration, but there was nothing.

The teacher smiled. "Now, hold the stone tightly and close your eyes."

"Okay." I closed my eyes.

"Clear your mind," said Ms. Benky in a soft voice.

You can do it, said Vee.

Oh, my God, get out of my head!

Vee didn't respond.

I sighed softly and tried concentrating on clearing my head, willing Vee *not* to interrupt.

"Now, open your eyes."

I did what she asked.

"Do you see anything?'

I looked at her. "Like what?"

Someone in the back snickered. I was pretty sure it was Megan.

"You must have been distracted," said the teacher. "Take a deep breath and try it again."

"Maybe someone else should give it a try," I replied.

"Nonsense. You can do this and when you see what the stones can do, you'll be blown away. Give it another try, Sara. You'll be glad that you did."

A little more intrigued, I did what she asked, this time trying to picture nothing but blackness in my head.

"Take deep breaths," said Ms. Benky in a soft, soothing voice. "And when you're ready, open your eyes."

After another minute, my eyes fluttered open and I couldn't believe what I was seeing. It was as if I'd stepped out of the classroom and into a beautiful, green meadow. As my eyes adjusted to the sunlight, I found that I was surrounded by vibrant, lush flowers, many of which I'd never seen before.

What do you see? asked Vee.

Beauty. Nature.

Birds chirped from the trees surrounding the meadow and a lone deer sipped water from a nearby stream. It raised its head and glanced my way, but from its calm stance, I couldn't tell if it really sensed me. After a few more seconds, it began walking in the opposite direction.

Smiling, I turned around and it was then that I found myself looking up at the biggest willow tree I'd ever seen. Drawn to it, I walked over and ducked my head, stepping under the elongated leaves. As I moved closer, my jaw dropped. There were hundreds of colorful, miniature homes hanging from the limbs of the giant tree. They were almost like bird houses, but much more intricately designed and beautiful. In the very center of everything was a magnificent white castle.

"Incredible," I whispered, wishing I could get a closer look. But the beautiful castle was well out of reach and something told me that my curious eyes wouldn't exactly be appreciated.

A flurry of noise startled me from beyond the tree. Before I knew what was happening, a swarm of fairies flew under the leaves and around me, toward their homes. They were tiny, even smaller than the elves, and they moved so fast that I couldn't get a clear view of what they truly looked like. Then, as if reading my mind, one small female stopped in front of me, hovering in the air, a friendly smile on her face.

"Can you see me?" I asked, staring back at the adorable little creature in awe. Clothed in a sparkly blue dress, she had long blonde hair, large green eyes, and pointy ears.

Instead of answering, the elf giggled and then zipped away from me, her iridescent wings flapping quickly as she disappeared into one of the homes.

What did you see? asked Vee.

You couldn't see it?

Vee didn't answer.

"Sara," called Ms. Benky, her voice sounding from far away. I felt her open my hand and then I was back in the classroom.

"Well?" asked Ms. Benky.

"It was... amazing," I said, still dazed by the experience. I already wanted to go back and see more.

"What was it like?" asked Emily, leaning forward in her seat, her eyes wide. "Did you see something?"

Before I could answer, Ms. Benky stopped me.

"Don't give anything away. It's too special," she said, touching my shoulder, her eyes twinkling. "And much more fun."

"Yes," I replied.

The teacher looked at the other students. "Don't worry, I'm going to give each of you a chance to experience what Sara just did. I only ask that you keep what you've seen to yourself until everyone has taken their turn."

Excited, they all agreed.

"Now, there are five stones. Each of you will get into groups of three and take a turn, say, three minutes a piece?" said the teacher, looking at the clock.

I went back to my desk and sat down. Megan looked at me, her eyebrow raised.

"It *was* really cool," I whispered, noticing that the other new girl, Dorie was also seated in the classroom. "That's all I'm going to say."

Looking bored, Megan sighed. "I guess I'll give it a whirl."

Afterward, even *she* was impressed with the vision.

"It was so realistic," Megan said, smiling at the teacher after taking her turn. "And one of them actually waved to me. Could they really see us?"

"Yes," replied Ms. Benky. "You probably looked to them more like some kind of an apparition. But the Fae definitely knew you were there."

"So, what we saw was real?" I asked.

"Yes. Definitely," she said.

"If humans are forbidden to step into their world, then why are they allowing us to see it?" asked another student.

"Mankind is growing and our natural resources are in turn, shrinking. Dramatically. Buildings go up and forests come down. If it keeps going on like this, the Fae will lose their home in that beautiful tree," replied the teacher. "I can't imagine how horrible it would be for them."

"So, they want our help?" asked Willow.

"They want to raise awareness. They can't do with the non-magic world, so we're their best shot," she said. "Which is why I've been gifted the stones."

"Why don't they just move their houses to a more remote forest? Like maybe somewhere in Alaska or even Wyoming?" asked Dorie.

"Even around here," said Megan. "In Canada."

The teacher frowned. "The tree is enchanted, for one. And, they've been living in it for centuries. Why should they have to relocate?"

"I want to help. They're so cute," said Emily. "And I can't imagine them being forced out of their homes."

We all agreed.

"Is that the only Fae kingdom?" asked Dorie.

"Yes," said Ms. Benky. "I've been told that there are other villages, but the Fae Queen lives in that tree."

The bell rang and the teacher's voice grew louder. "Tomorrow we will be talking about fairy dust, by the way."

"Do you have some?" asked Dorie, looking excited.

"You'll find out tomorrow," said Ms. Benky, winking.

"I love this school already," said Dorie, as we filed out of class. "What about you guys?"

"It's not so bad, I guess," said Megan, still sounding bored. Something told me that she'd never admit to how much she liked the class, only because she'd been forced into it.

"I loved the class," said Willow. "I can't wait to get to my next one."

"What is it?" asked Dorie.

Willow looked down at her schedule. "It's Potions."

"Oh, I have Potions, too," I said, holding up my slip of paper.

Dorie squealed. "I have that class too! Can I walk with you?"

"Uh, sure," said Willow, giving me a sideways look.

"Yeah, no problem," I said, noticing how busy the hallways were now. A lot of the other students watched us as we walked past them. Some smiled and others just stared curiously.

"Good. If we get lost, at least we won't be alone," said Dorie.

"Very true. I'd hate to get lost in this school. Did you see any of the poltergeists?" said Willow, as we all stopped in front of the restroom.

Dorie's eyes widened. "They have poltergeists?"

"Yes. Just don't interact with them or you'll regret it. Darn, I have Herbal Medicine," said Megan, frowning down at her schedule. "Sounds... thrilling."

"So do I," said Kendra. "We'll walk together."

"Sure. I wonder where your Room Advisor is. Little Miss Candy Cane," said Megan, stuffing her schedule back into her robe with a smirk.

"She hates being called Candy," I said in a low voice. "Don't antagonize her."

"Here I am," said Candace, popping out of nowhere. "And she's right, you call me Candy one more time, and I'll not only tell the poltergeists your room number, but I'll have Sherry invite them to work out with you."

Megan's lips tightened. "You wouldn't."

"If you're going to keep picking on me, I certainly will," said the elf, jutting her chin out.

"I'm not trying to pick on you" said Megan, looking surprised. "And I guess I didn't realize how much you hated being called Candy."

"I hate it almost as much as I hate trolls," she said.

"Wow. Okay, well, I won't ever call you it again. Peace?" said Megan.

Candace relaxed and managed to even smile. "Yes. Peace."

"Don't mind M... Ava," said Kendra, catching herself quickly. "It's just her way. We've even learned to ignore it, most of the time."

"Kendra is right. I'm a little snarky at times, but I'm like that with everyone," said Megan.

"I'm not used to being around cynical people, so I'll try and remember that," said Candace.

"I'm not cynical," argued Megan.

"Oh, please," said Kendra. "Don't even try arguing that."

Megan blushed. "I'm not. I'm a realist."

A witch that's a realist, mocked Vee. *Now I've heard everything.*

I smiled.

"Why is that funny?" asked Megan, noticing.

"I wasn't smiling about you. I was smiling because Candace and you are so opposite, it's funny," I lied, even though it was true.

"So true," said Kendra.

"What's that supposed to mean?" asked Megan.

"Candace is like a little cheerleader. She's excited about life and pumped for... everything. Then there's you," I said. "I've never known you to be excited about anything other than... that boyfriend you have, back in Bayport."

Megan stared at me in surprise. "Wow, where did that come from?"

"Oh, come on. Like it's not the truth," I said.

"I'm excited about things. Just not anything here," said Megan. "And I wouldn't talk. You weren't exactly thrilled about going to this school either, Kala."

"The name is Sara," I said tightly.

"That's what I meant," she replied, glaring at me.

"We should really get to class," said Kendra, nudging Megan.

"Yes. It's getting late. Do you know where you're going?" asked Candace.

"I think we can find them," I replied.

Candace smiled. "Oh, that's good. I have some errands to run for Dean Marigold, otherwise I'd accompany you."

"It's not a problem," said Kendra. "Do what you have to do. We'll find our way."

"Thanks. I will see you around lunchtime," said Candace, before disappearing.

"She's certainly sensitive," said Megan, as we started walking again.

She should talk, said Vee.

"Very. In fact, I think Candy is a cute name. I can't believe she got so bent out of shape because of it," said Dorie. "Which reminds me, what did you say your names were again?"

"They are right here listed on our robes," said Megan, looking down at hers. "I'm...Ava."

Dorie snorted. "Are you sure about that?"

"What is that supposed to mean?" asked Megan, stopping abruptly.

Dorie's cheeks turned pink. "Nothing."

Megan sighed. "Sorry. I'm just tired from lack of sleep."

"I hear that. I didn't get a lot of sleep last night either," replied Dorie.

"Where did you say you're from?" asked Willow, staring at her face. "I swear, you look so familiar."

"I'm from Wisconsin. I doubt we've ever met," she replied quickly.

"Where in Wisconsin?" ask Willow.

"The area where they grow most of their cheese," joked Dorie.

Willow gave her a confused look.

"I'm kidding. I'm from Madison," said Dorie. "Have you ever been there?"

"No," replied Willow.

Dorie smiled. "I didn't think so." She looked at Kendra. "So are you all rooming together?"

"I'm rooming with Sara," my sister replied, nodding toward me. "And those two share a room."

"I'm rooming alone for now. Talk about boring. We should hang out. After classes are over," said Dorie.

"I'm going straight to bed after my last class," said Megan, yawning. "You all can do what you want."

"There's the Potions room," I said as we approached it. I glanced back at Kendra and Megan. "Have fun in Herbal Medicine."

Megan snorted.

"See ya," called Kendra, as they headed away.

I had to admit – Potions class was interesting. We even learned how to make something that stopped the hiccups.

"It's important that you get your formula right or you'll create something that will make one unable to get rid of the hiccups. For life," said Ms. Hotchkins, her expression grave. "And believe me, I've *seen* it happen. It's not good."

After the bell rang, Ms. Hotchkins pulled Dorie aside.

"I'll catch up to you guys," she called out to me and Willow as we were heading out the door.

"Looks like we have a new friend," I said, in the hallway. "Not sure if that's good. When we leave, she's going to be bummed out."

"Yeah. You're probably right. Maybe we should put some distance between us?" asked Willow.

"I don't want her to think we're snobs but I don't know what other choice we really have," I replied as we caught up to Kendra and Megan.

"What are you talking about?" asked Megan.

"Dorie. She's nice and all, but we can't afford to get too close to her, you know?" I replied.

"I agree," said Kendra. "Befriending us is a bad idea. It could even be dangerous."

"Now who's being cynical?" said Megan.

"Actually, I'm being a realist," said Kendra dryly. "You should recognize that."

Megan smirked.

"How was your class?" I asked, wanting to change the subject. Everyone was tired and testy, which wasn't making the day go by any easier.

"It was actually interesting," said Kendra. "We learned the many uses of elder."

"Elder? Never heard of it," I said.

"It's an antiviral medicine. You can use the flowers, the fruit, and the bark for different medicinal uses," said Kendra. She held up a sample of the plant in a plastic baggie, and I noticed that there were little black berries. "You can also make wine, jam, or paint with the fruit."

"Cool," I said. "Is that what you're planning on doing?"

"Maybe someday," she said, stuffing it into her robe. "Everyone got a free sample. It's just good to have around."

"Crap, here comes Dorie," murmured Megan, looking back over her shoulder.

"Hey guys! Wait up," called the witch, waving at us from down the hallway.

We stopped walking.

Dorie raced to catch up with us. "Where's your next class?" she asked, looking slightly winded.

"I have 'Ins and Outs of Dark Arts'," I said.

"So do I," she replied, excitedly.

The others had White Magic and Mayhem, which sounded interesting, but I was actually looking forward to my class.

"Let's walk together," said Dorie.

"Sure." I turned and looked at Kala. "The schedule says that we have lunch after this. I'll meet you in the cafeteria?"

"Okay," she said.

I glanced at Dorie. "It looks like our class is on a different level."

Looking down at the schedule, she nodded. "It is. What does DNG stand for, I wonder?"

"The dungeon," said Emily, stopping next to us. "Are you heading to the 'Ins and Outs of Dark Arts'? That's where I'm going."

"Yes. *We* are," I said, nodding toward Dorie.

"Cool. I'll show you where it is," said the redhead.

We said goodbye to the others and followed Emily toward one of the elevators.

"So, where are you two from?" she asked us when we were inside.

"I'm from Wisconsin," said Dorie.

"Really? That's where I'm from," said Emily. "Which city?"

"Uh, Madison," said Dorie, looking suddenly uncomfortable.

"Oh. I'm from Milwaukee. What about you?" she asked, turning toward me.

"My cousin and I are from Florida," I said, forcing a smile to my face.

"Really? I bet you've been to Disneyworld a few times then, huh? I've always wanted to go there," said Emily.

"Oh yeah," I lied. "It's been a long time since we've been there, though. Couldn't tell you what the new attractions are."

Emily smiled. "It's okay."

"So, what's this class like?" asked Dorie. "Are we going to learn some wicked spells?"

Emily sighed. "No. It's actually kind of boring. Right now, we're learning the history of bonding wands. When they were first created and stuff like that."

"Bonding wands? Really?" I said, perking up. *What were the chances of that?* "Neat. Do you have one?"

"A bonding wand? No... they're hard to come by. In fact, the teacher thinks there are only four or five left in the world. Many have been destroyed."

"Wow, really? They must be pretty powerful then, huh?" I asked.

"Yes. Three in particular. It's said that if you possessed them, you could basically take over the world," said Emily. "And nobody could stop you."

"That's... wild," I said. "So, which one is the most powerful? The dark one?"

Emily's eyes widened. "How did you know there was a dark one?"

I felt myself breaking out into a cold sweat. "I just assumed there was. Since the class is about the dark arts."

"Duh," said Emily, chuckling. "I guess that would make sense. There's also one for White magic though, too."

"You said there were three of them all together," said Dorie. "What of the third?"

"It's used for undoing what the other wands have done, so technically, it's a neutral wand," said Emily.

"So, it's a wand that can be used for Black or White, basically. Right?" asked Dorie.

"I am not sure if it works that way but it's supposed to reverse any spell that the other two wands can create. If you ask me, *that's* a wand I'd love to get a hold of," said Emily.

"You and me both," said Dorie, staring off into space.

CHAPTER SIXTEEN

Beldora

The girls rode down the elevator in silence, with two other girls, who were chatting away. Meanwhile, Beldora had to stop herself from tackling Kala so she could search for Penelope. The task was already taking much longer than anticipated.

At least I now know which sister has the dark one, she thought.

All she had to do was bide a little more time and wait for the right opportunity to steal the wand. If that proved too difficult, she would go after Willow's.

AKA Laina.

It was obvious the Asian girl was Opal's daughter. Ava was too cocky and the other blonde was rooming with Kala. She had to be Kendra.

"Long elevator ride, huh?" said Emily.

"Yeah," replied Kendra.

Beldora nodded, her mind on other things. And not just the wands. She also now wanted the enchanted Fae stones. She knew a half-troll who would pay a pretty penny to get his hands on something that might lead him to their kingdom. She wasn't sure why he hated the Fae so much, but it had something to do with being double-crossed by their queen.

When girls finally arrived at their destination, Beldora took a seat next to Kala and stared in appreciation at some of the artifacts that were displayed throughout the classroom.

"Wow, is that a wizard's staff?" asked Kala, pointing to a glass case.

"Yes," said Emily, who was seated on the other side of her. "It belonged to Marwick."

Beldora's jaw dropped.

"Who was Marwick?" asked Kala.

Emily explained. "Marwick was a legendary evil sorcerer who had once destroyed an entire kingdom after being snubbed by the King's daughter. He was later killed by another, more powerful sorcerer, Danube, the man the princess had sworn her true love to. He was also Marwick's younger brother. In the end, it was said that Danube had died of a broken heart."

"That's so sad," said Kala, frowning. "Do you think it was true?"

"I'm not sure. How tragic though, huh?" said Emily.

"Yes," said Kala. "So many people hurt, too. It's really sad."

"Do you have a boyfriend?" asked Emily.

Kala smiled. "Well, kind of. I mean, we're seeing each other."

"What's his name?" asked Emily, resting her chin on the palm of her hand.

"Ba–" Kala stopped.

"Ba?" repeated Emily.

"Barry," said Kala, smiling.

"Barry, huh?" asked Beldora. She knew exactly who Kala was seeing. It was Bailey, the meddling shape-shifter. "Where'd you meet him?"

"At the beach," she said, running a hand through her long, dark hair, a faraway look in her eyes. "He's a lifeguard."

Lying witch.

"Sounds interesting," said Emily, smiling. "Is he cute?"

"I think so," said Kala, before the teacher called for their attention.

***

Surprisingly, "The Ins and Outs of Dark Arts" gave Beldora a new respect for the three bonding wands. At the end of class, she vowed that no matter what happened, she needed to get *both* Kala's and Willow's wands before returning to Salem. She would still try and use Penelope to free Vivian, but she'd keep Juniper for herself. A wand like that would guarantee her safety, which is something she'd need when and if Vivian was set free. Although they needed her at the moment, she knew that the woman wasn't playing with a full deck of cards and certainly wasn't trustworthy. For all Beldora knew, Vivian was already considering snuffing them out as soon as she escaped the globe. With Juniper in her possession, Vivian couldn't succeed.

"So, what did you think?" she asked Kala.

"About the class?"

"Yeah, and the story about the bonding wands?"

"It was very interesting," she answered.

"I wish I had one. Mine is just… average," said Beldora, pulling it out of her robe. She held it up. "I'm not even sure what it's made of. What about yours?"

"My wand?" asked Kala.

Beldora smiled innocently. "Yes. Can I see it?"

Kala shrugged and pulled it out of her robe. "To be honest, I'm really not sure myself."

Beldora stared at the wand in shock but then reminded herself that the wretched girl wouldn't be stupid enough to take her real wand out in public.

"That looks like it's made out of ebony wood," said Emily, walking next to them again. "Mine is made out of wenge." She pulled her wand out. "Who knows what's in the core, though. I'd be interested in finding out."

"The core?" asked Kala.

"Yes. The core is what makes it magic. It can be anything from unicorn hair to dragon claw," explained Emily.

"That's true, but what truly makes the wands magical are the spells used when creating one," said Beldora, not even sure why she was educating the twits.

"It's a combination of the spell and the core ingredients," corrected Emily.

Miss Know-It-All.

Beldora could feel her eye twitch. "Obviously, that's what I meant."

Emily smiled. "I'm sure you did."

When they reached the elevator, it was filling up quickly.

"There's room for another," said one of the girls, moving over.

"Go ahead," said Kala, looking at Beldora.

"Thanks. I'm in a hurry anyway. Have to stop at my room and make sure my luggage made it," she replied, getting in quickly. "See you in the lunchroom."

The elevator door closed before the other witches could respond.

When she reached her desired floor, Beldora rushed out of the elevator and sought out Sybil, who was eating lunch at her desk.

"That new girl, Sara, asked me to meet her at her room, so we could walk to the lunchroom together. I forgot which number it is. Can you help me?"

Sybil looked up from her sandwich. "Oh good. You're making friends already."

"Yes. She's very nice."

"Let me check the system and I'll tell you," said Sybil, opening up her laptop. She began typing. "Hmm... I'm not finding anything. I bet Marigold doesn't have it entered into the system yet."

"Oh no," pouted Beldora. "She's going to think I'm standing her up."

"Can't you just meet her in the cafeteria?"

"No. She might spend all day waiting for me and never make it to the cafeteria. Isn't there any other way to find out where her room is?"

"Let me check with her House Advisor. I know Candace was assigned to her," she said, pulling out her wand. She waved it and the elf appeared.

"Hi. What can I help you with?" asked Candace.

"Could you show Dorie to Sara's room? The new girl?" asked Sybil. "They're supposed to meet for lunch."

"Of course," said the elf.

"Just tell me which room she's in," said Beldora. "I'll find it myself."

"Are you sure? I'm not busy at the moment," said Candace.

"I can find it," said Beldora firmly, trying to remain calm.

The elf told her.

"And where is Willow's room?"

Both elf and witch gave her a blank look.

"Sorry, I meant Laina," she said and then laughed. "I'm still thinking of that Fae willow tree. It was beautiful. Have you actually seen it before, Candace?"

"Yes," replied the elf, her face lighting up. "I'm friends with a few of the Fae and have visited their kingdom many times. My village isn't too far away, either."

"You're so lucky. I wish that I could see your village. I bet it's just as magical," said Beldora.

"It's not quite as glamorous as the Fae's, but I love it," said Candace, a faraway look in her eyes.

"You'll have to tell me about it sometime. When there's more time," said Beldora.

"Sure. If you'd like," said the elf.

"Goodness, I need to get going," said Beldora, staring up at the clock. "Where did you say Laina's room was?"

"Her room is across the hall. Why?" asked Candace.

"She asked me to grab her hairbrush," said Beldora, smiling widely. "Since I was meeting with Sara anyway."

"Oh. Okay," said Candace, not really having any reason to doubt her. "You sure you don't want my help?"

"No, but thank you," she replied, heading for the door.

"How's your first day going?" called out Sybil.

"Great. Thanks for asking," she said loudly, racing toward the doorway.

And it's about to get a whole lot better...

Less than five minutes later, she was inside of Kendra and Kala's room. With her heart pounding in her chest, Beldora began searching through the girl's things, frantic to find the wands so she could get back to Salem.

"What are you doing?"

Startled, Beldora turned around and noticed Candace standing behind her. The look on her face spoke volumes.

So, the elf isn't as clueless as she appears...

"I'm waiting for Sara."

"It looks like you're doing more than that," said the elf, her hands on her waist. She nodded toward the open drawers of the dresser. "In fact, it looks to me like you're going through their things."

"I don't have time for this," mumbled Beldora.

"You're going to have to come with me to the dean's office," said the elf. "Ms. Weiss will want to know about this."

"Fine," she answered. "Let's go."

Instead of following her, however, Beldora quickly pulled out her wand and cast a dark spell on Candace. One that put her into a deep sleep while also making her forget what she'd walked in on. The little elf crumbled to the floor and began snoring soundly.

Satisfied, Beldora continued looking through Kala's room, mumbling to herself. After a few minutes, she spotted the walk-in closet and hurried inside. Looking around, she still found nothing. Frustrated, she growled in her throat.

What if they left the wands somewhere in Bayport?

Hoping she was wrong, and trying to remain calm, Beldora turned on her heel to leave the closet, when she noticed one of the floor panels wasn't quite level with the rest. She got down on her knees and smiled as the piece of wood lifted easily.

"There you are," said Beldora, after opening up one of the hand towels she'd found hidden inside.

It was Chloe.

Her hand shook as she wrapped the wand back up, careful not to touch the wood. When she found the second wand, Beldora's smile widened.

Penelope.

Elated, Beldora almost grabbed the handle of the wand when she remembered herself.

Fool, you almost got yourself killed, she told herself.

She needed Juniper.

In the class she'd just stepped out of, Beldora had learned that Juniper wasn't deadly. Either the wand worked with you or it wouldn't work at all. It didn't inflict death. It would just ignore you, which, for some arrogant witches, was almost as bad.

Beldora quickly wrapped the second wand up and rushed out the door, to the room across the hall. After several minutes of searching, she found Juniper under one of the beds, also hidden beneath a floorboard. Feeling victorious, she waved her own wand, straightening out the mess she'd made of both rooms, and then headed back to Salem.

CHAPTER SEVENTEEN

Kala

I met back up with Kendra, Willow, and Megan outside of the cafeteria. As we stepped into the lunch line, Megan asked me about Dorie.

"I don't know where she is. She mentioned something about meeting us here," I replied.

"We really need to separate ourselves from her," reminded Kendra. "Oh look. They're having pizza today. I wonder if it's as gross as the stuff we have back at our old school."

"Probably," I replied, grabbing an empty tray and sliding it across the metal counter.

"I don't know. I think it looks pretty good," said Willow.

"You've never had school food before," said Megan. "It's usually pretty nasty. Most of it, at least."

The food being offered consisted of pizza, mixed vegetables, spaghetti and meatballs, garlic toast, and some kind of chocolate cake. There was also a fruit and salad plate. Each item was displayed behind a glass enclosure and unlike back home, where the lunch was served by actual people, there wasn't anyone around to help us.

"What do we do?" asked Willow.

The girl in front of me, Amy, looked over her shoulder at us. "You just point to what you want or say what it is, and it will appear on your tray."

"Sweet," said Megan. "What about beverages?"

"Same thing," said the girl. "There's milk, water, or juice. They also have almond or soy milk."

"Figures," grumbled Megan. "What I wouldn't do for a can of soda."

"What about coffee?" I asked. "Do they have that?"

"Since when do you drink coffee?" asked Kendra.

I shrugged. "It would be great to have something to wake us up. We still have a few hours left before school is out."

"There isn't any coffee but there's tea," said Amy. "I forgot to mention that."

"Thanks," I said. "Tea it is then."

"So, how do you like the school so far?" asked Amy, as we were selecting our food.

"It's very... interesting. Better than regular school, I guess," I replied.

"Where are you from?" she asked.

I was about to say Bayport and caught myself. "My cousin and I are from Florida," I said, nodding back toward Kala. "And those two are originally from Sweden."

Amy's eyebrows rose. "Really? They don't have accents."

"No we don't," said Megan loudly. "We lost them a while ago. Our parents travel a lot."

"You two are sisters?" asked Amy, her eyes shifting from Willow to Megan.

"Yeah. Step-sisters," said Megan. "My mother married her father. That's why we look so different."

I made a mental note to tell Megan not to make such a big deal about their differences. She looked too anxious, and maybe a little angry, explaining the situation.

"How long have you been here?" I asked the girl, changing the subject.

"Two years now. I'm graduating next year," Amy replied.

"So, you're in eleventh grade?" I asked.

"No, it's different here. They don't go by grades, they go by courses. You get so many credits and then you graduate. I already have my high school diploma. I received it last year," she explained.

"So, when you graduate here, you get some kind of a magic degree?" asked Kendra.

"Yes. You can continue your education, however, if you plan on teaching magic; they have special programs," she answered.

"Really?" asked Willow, looking excited. "I would love to be a teacher. How many more years of schooling do you need to become one?"

"At least four years. Most of the training is done outside of the school. You travel abroad and train with some of the most powerful sorcerers and sorceresses around."

Even I had to admit, it sounded exciting.

"Thanks for the information," said Kendra.

"No problem," said Amy.

"Yes, thank you," said Willow. "This is so exciting, I'm going to have to talk to my mother about all of this."

"I'm sure *our* mother will be very interested in all of this," said Megan, staring at Willow hard.

"Err... yes," said Willow, looking flushed. "Maybe we can both take teaching courses?"

Megan snorted. "No way. School and I don't fly."

Amy giggled. "You *will* fly. Brooms One-O-One."

"I can't wait to fly," said Willow. "Back in Salem–"

"You've been to Salem?" asked Amy.

"Yes. Just to visit," said Megan quickly.

"That's where I'm originally from," said Amy. "In fact, my great aunt is a coven leader there."

"What's her name?" I asked.

"Meredith."

Willow opened her mouth to say something and I gave her a warning look.

"Well, it was nice talking to you," said Amy, picking up her tray. "I'll see you around."

"Goodbye," I said.

"Close one," muttered Kendra under her breath.

"Sorry," whispered Willow. "I forgot."

"It's okay," I said as we walked toward the back of the cafeteria to an empty table. "No harm done. I'm sure we've all made mistakes today."

"Yeah," said Kendra. "But, obviously, we're still doing fine. We haven't been found out, the day is half over, and our wands are safe and sound."

"There is that," I said. Little did we know that it wasn't really the case.

CHAPTER EIGHTEEN

Beldora

"You have all three wands?" repeated Bella, staring at her in disbelief. "How did you pull that off?"

"It took me a few hours but I got them," replied Beldora, unable to wipe the grin from her face. "I almost got my hands on some enchanted Fae stones as well, but I didn't want to risk staying there any longer."

"What do you mean? What are they and what do they do?" asked Bella.

Beldora explained what had happened during the Enchanted Objects class.

"It was like we were right there," said Beldora. "In the Fae kingdom."

"That troll, Egra, would pay an arm and a leg for those stones. You realize that, don't you?" said Bella.

"I know but it's too dangerous to go back. Once they find out that the wands are missing, and I'm no longer there, they'll know it was me," she replied.

"I suppose," said Bella, carefully opening up the hand towels with the wands. "Now, which of these can we hold?"

"Juniper is safe. Not the others."

Bella looked up at her. "Are you sure about that?"

"Not one hundred percent. But, today we learned about the bonding wands in another class, and the teacher thought it was possible."

"She *thought*," scoffed Bella.

"We could always test it out on someone."

"There isn't time. Besides, what if they don't give it back?"

Beldora sighed. "True."

"Which one of these wands is Juniper?" asked Bella.

She pointed. "That's the one I found in Willow's room. Don't you recognize it?"

"It looks familiar." She laughed nervously. "I'm just terrified of touching the wrong wand."

"That's Juniper. I know it is."

"Okay," she said, holding her hand over it.

"Just pick it up."

Bella arched an eyebrow. "Why don't *you* pick it up?"

She took a deep breath. "Fine. I will. Just so you know, if the bonding wand accepts me I'm not giving it up, though," said Beldora, lowering her voice. "Obviously, I will release her from the globe, but I deserve the wand. Especially after everything I've been through today."

Bella's eyes narrowed. Wanting the wand herself, she snatched it from the table.

"Hey," snapped Beldora angrily. "What's the deal?"

"We don't have all day," said Bella, waiting for some kind of sign that the wand was willing to accept her. "You were taking too long."

"Just remember – *I'm* the one who's done most of the work. I deserve Juniper," pouted Beldora.

"Stop talking so I can concentrate," said Bella, closing her eyes.

After several seconds, Beldora tapped her on the shoulder. "Anything?"

"No. Not yet. Let me be," replied Bella, irritated.

Sighing, Beldora walked over to the globe and told Vivian that they'd be freeing her soon.

Vivian pointed toward Bella, who still had her eyes closed and was mumbling something. She shook her head and then pointed to Beldora.

"Me?" she mouthed.

Vivian nodded quickly.

Beldora turned back toward Bella. "I don't think it's willing to accept you. Let me try."

"No. Not yet," said Bella. "Just give it a few more minutes."

Beldora crossed her arms and began tapping her foot.

"Stop that racket," muttered Bella, opening one eye.

"You know, Vivian thinks the wand will bond with me," said Beldora, raising her chin.

Bella opened both eyes. "Why?"

"I don't know but if the wand wanted you, it would have bonded by now."

Bella gritted her teeth. "Fine," she said, holding the wand out. "Go for it."

Beldora grabbed the wand, but there was nothing.

"Do you feel anything?" asked Bella, watching her carefully.

"No," she mumbled. "I don't even know what I'm supposed to feel, if you want to know the truth."

"Give it more time."

After a few minutes, Beldora gave up.

"What now?" asked Bella.

"You tell me," she replied, dropping the wand onto the table angrily. "I'm out of ideas."

"We should ask Vivian."

Beldora walked back over to the globe. "It didn't work. What do we do now?"

Vivian began to pace back and forth. After several seconds, she stopped and said something to Mark. He nodded and began spraying paint into the snow.

"Opal," read Bella.

"Opal won't help us," said Beldora.

"She will if we threaten her with something," said Bella, an idea forming in her head. "In fact, we'll tell her that we have Willow and that the girl will die if she doesn't help us."

"What if she doesn't believe us?"

Bella waved her hand at the wand. "We have Willow's wand. Why wouldn't she? In fact, we have all of the wands. She'd be stupid not to realize that we have the upper hand."

"Good point. Do you know where Opal is?" asked Beldora.

"I think she's at Adrianne's," said Bella. "That's where I saw her last."

"Then let's get over there and grab her," said Beldora, looking exhausted. "So we can finally get this over with."

***

Finding Opal turned out to be much easier than they'd anticipated.

"I told you she was here," whispered Bella, as they stared at Willow's mother through the bushes. Opal was in Adrianne's backyard, seated at a picnic table, and reading some kind of romance book

"I wonder where Adrianne is?" said Beldora, looking around the yard anxiously.

"Probably looking for us," said Bella. "Now, go over and tell Opal that you're friends with the girls and try to draw her away from the yard."

"Me? Why me?" asked Beldora nervously.

"Because you're still a teenager and she'd obviously recognize me," said Bella, wondering how Beldora was able to get her hands on the prized wands when she was such a scatterbrain. "Think about it."

Beldora let out an exasperated sigh. "Fine. If you see Adrianne, Clarice, or any of the others, you'd better back me up."

"Of course I will," said Bella. "Now, go and get her."

Running a hand through her hair, Beldora walked around the hedge and approached Opal.

"Hello?" said Opal, stiffening up.

Beldora laughed as if she was a nervous teenager. "Um, hi. I live next door and... I think Kala's cat is on our roof again," Beldora said, proud of herself for coming up with the excuse on such short notice.

"Cat? I didn't know she owned a cat," said Opal, putting her book down onto the picnic table.

"Yes. It's a Tabby. Her name is Precious. Can you let Kala know so she can help me get her down? The poor cat looks terrified."

"I'll help you. Kala is out of town," said Opal, getting up.

"Thank you," said Beldora, smiling as she led her away from Adrianne's. "I know you're going to be very helpful."

"We'll see," said Opal. "I'm not sure what I can do to get her down, but I'll try my best."

"Yes, you will try your best," said Bella, stepping around the corner, smiling darkly.

Opal tried to run, but Beldora grabbed her arm and transported the both of them to Salem.

CHAPTER NINETEEN

Vivian

"They found her," said Vivian, smiling up at Bella and Beldora, who were pointing toward their captive. Opal had tears running down her face and was pleading with them to let her go. "The knuckleheads may actually pull this off."

"What if she can't use the wand?" asked Mark, not looking very confident.

"Don't be such a pessimist. Her daughter was able to bond with Juniper. Chances are that Opal will be able to as well." Vivian gave them two thumbs up.

"Still."

"Just cross your fingers and hope for the best."

"I'm hoping for a miracle," he muttered as Bella and Beldora threatened to kill Willow if Opal didn't cooperate.

"Hopefully she's closer to her daughter than I am to mine," mused Vivian, watching.

Believing that Willow's life was in danger, Opal reluctantly accepted the wand. She picked it up and a light began to radiate from the wand and into her.

"It's working," squealed Vivian happily.

Mark smiled. "Thank goodness."

"Goodness had nothing to do with this," said Vivian, her pulse now racing. She was about to be freed from the globe. Something she'd been dreaming about for weeks. It felt surreal.

The light began to dissipate and they listened as Bella ordered Opal to say the words that would undo the spell.

"Not until I see my daughter," said Opal stubbornly.

"Bring her Willow's hand," said Bella to Beldora. She grinned wickedly. "She only needs one. Wait, which hand does she write with, Opal? We'll spare that one."

Opal stared at her in horror. "No! Don't you dare hurt my child, you monster!"

"Then free Vivian and Mark or she'll not only be hurt, she'll be dead," snapped Bella. "After all, we don't really need her. We need you."

"If you kill her I will never help you," said Opal, glaring at her.

"And if you don't help us, we'll just kill everyone," said Bella, pointing toward the other two wands which sat on the table. They were wrapped in towels, but Opal recognized them right away. "As you can see, we have both Kendra's and Kala's wands as well."

"Where are the girls?" asked Opal, feeling faint. Everything seemed so hopeless.

"I can't tell you that, but mark my words, if you don't free Vivian, then you'll never see any of the girls alive again."

"Please, don't you dare hurt them."

"We'll let them go. But only if you do what we ask. I promise you," said Bella.

"What of her?" asked Opal, nodding toward the globe. "Will *she* let everyone go?"

Vivian nodded vehemently and then clasped her hands together, begging to be let out of the globe.

"Why should I trust any of you?" asked Opal.

"Why should you not? We have the girls. We have their wands. You can either help us or die. But not before we make you watch us kill your precious daughter and those other two brats."

"How did you find them?" asked Opal.

"Come on now. Did you really think hiding the girls at The Roix was really that ingenious? It was easy and as you can see, our very own Beldora fit right in," said Bella, waving a hand toward her.

Beldora, with a smug smile, curtsied.

"Fine," said Opal. "Tell me what to do."

"I think all she really has to do is point Juniper toward the globe and say 'Reverse Penelope's Spell'. That's it," said Beldora, remembering what she'd learned earlier in class. It was an easy phrase that the wand maker had created for Margaritte, the first owner of Juniper.

Opal took a deep breath and repeated the words. A yellow light shot out of the end of the wand and into the globe. There was a blinding light and then a loud cracking noise. When the witches opened their eyes, standing before them was Vivian and Mark, both free from their prison and covered in snow.

"We did it!" cried Bella, clapping her hands together. She laughed out loud. "I can't believe it."

"Neither can I," said Vivian, shaking off the snow. "Well done."

"She and Mark are free," said Opal miserably. "I did what you asked. Now… where are the girls?"

Bella and Beldora looked at Vivian, not sure what to do next.

Opal clenched her jaw. "Tell me or… I'll reverse the spell I just reversed."

"Can she do that?" asked Bella, her smile gone.

Vivian stared at Opal, surprised at her show of moxie. "To be honest, I really don't know."

"No, you don't, but I know more about this wand than any of you," said Opal, backing away from them. "It was my mother's. Now, tell me exactly where Willow and the others are, or I swear to God, I'll put you back where you came from."

"Just tell her," said Vivian. "She'll find out anyway soon enough."

"Neither of the girls are here," said Bella. "They're still at the school. Safe and sound. Now, give me the wand back."

"You tricked me?" asked Opal, staring at her in horror.

"Of course we did," said Bella, smirking. "You're extremely gullible, so it was quite easy."

Opal glanced at Kala's and Kendra's wands again. Above all else, she knew that Vivian mustn't get her hands on Penelope. Trying not to raise suspicions, Opal began moving toward the other two wands slowly. "The three of you are despicable," she said. "I don't know how you can even live with yourselves."

"Don't be so dramatic. Now, put the wand down and leave," said Vivian, getting angry. "Before you get hurt."

"I'm not the one who needs to worry about getting hurt," said Opal. "So don't you threaten *me*."

"Mark, take the wand from her," ordered Vivian.

Before he could react, Opal jumped into action. She snatched the other two wands, chanted a spell, and vanished.

"You've got to be kidding me!" raged Vivian.

"She has all three wands!" cried Beldora.

"Yes, because you fools just left them sitting out in the open," screamed Vivian, furious. "Go and find them!"

"Where could she have taken them?" asked Beldora.

"Back to Bayport, you idiot," said Vivian, glaring at her. "Where else?"

"Or to The Roix, so she can return the wands to Kendra and Kala," said Mark

"You'd better find her before that happens," ordered Vivian. "Now!"

CHAPTER TWENTY

Kala

Willow, Megan, Kendra, and I were on our way to our last class of the day, when the dean materialized before us.

"Come with me. Now," she ordered.

"Where?" I asked. frowning.

"My office."

"What's going on?" asked Kendra.

Marigold glanced around the hallway nervously. "You'll know soon enough, and watch out for Dorie. She isn't who you think she is."

"What do you mean? Wo is she?" asked Megan.

"Beldora," she replied in a low voice.

We all gasped in shock.

"Come along. Quickly," she said and began walking.

As we followed her, Marigold exchanged greetings with several of the students, putting on a happy face even though it was obvious that something was very wrong. When we arrived back in her office, we were all shocked to find Adrianne waiting for us there.

"Mom, what are you doing here?" asked Kendra.

"We have to get you out of the school. Vivian has been released from the globe," she replied, looking exhausted.

"How?" I asked, frowning.

"Beldora stole your wands," she answered.

I gasped. "She has *all* of them?"

"Apparently," said Adrianne.

"Even mine?" asked Willow.

"Yes. It's how she was able to free Vivian," she replied.

"But how on earth did she find them?" asked Willow.

"I'm not exactly sure, but we need to leave," she answered. "Marigold said you can keep the wands she gave you earlier. Use them now."

We pulled our wands out of our pockets.

"Where to?" I asked.

"A place where nobody would expect to find you. My parents' cabin in Salem," she answered.

"Why can't we just go to Vail?" asked Kendra.

Adrianne paused and then said. "It's too dangerous. Opal might have told Vivian about the place."

"What do you mean?" asked Willow.

"They kidnapped her because they needed someone who could operate Juniper. Your mother was able to," she replied. "But don't worry, Opal got away. She also stole back your wands. You should be proud of her."

Willow sighed in relief. "I am."

"Come on, girls. We really need to go. Vivian is in a tizzy and wants her wand back. Even more so, she wants revenge," said Adrianne. "We need to get you somewhere safe."

"Good luck," said Marigold. "And let me know if I can be of more help."

"You've already done plenty," said Adrianne, smiling. "And will be rewarded fittingly."

Marigold smiled sadly. "Just put Vivian back into that globe. That's the only reward I want."

"We'll do our best," said Adrianne.

"How do we find your parents' cabin?" I asked, preparing to leave.

"It's near the big tree. The Tree of Death. We'll meet there and then I'll show you where the cabin is," she said, raising her wand. She disappeared and we soon followed.

CHAPTER TWENTY-ONE

Kala

When we arrived at the tree, Adrianne led us to the cabin, which was only a two-minute hike.

"This is where you lived growing up?" I asked as we stepped onto the porch. It was larger than the other cabins we'd seen but even more rundown. From the way the paint had peeled and the amount of weeds there were, it was obvious that the place had been abandoned long ago.

"Yes," she answered, holding the door open for us. "Charming, isn't it?"

"Nobody else is living here?" asked Kendra.

"No. Our family still owns the cabin. It's never been sold," she explained.

We all stepped inside.

"What's going on?" I said, stopping in my tracks. Mark, Bella, and Beldora were all there, wands raised.

Adrianne snatched my wand away and then pointed it at us. "Sit down. All of you."

Kendra's eyes narrowed. "Vivian."

"Bingo. Now sit your butts down on the couch," she replied sharply.

"Go," I said to the others, ignoring her. Vivian had my wand but not theirs and they had a chance. "Tell Mom and the others what's happening."

Vivian laughed and then grabbed my arm. "Yes. Good idea. Go and tell your 'mom' and her cronies all about it. By the way, which one are you?" she asked, eyeing me curiously.

I just glared at her.

"That's Kala," said Beldora, who was now back to her old self and no longer a teen.

"Perfect," said Vivian. "Go and tell the others that I have Kala, and if Opal doesn't give me my wand back, they'll never see her again."

Kendra raised her wand. "Let her go."

Vivian laughed again. "Or what? You're going to turn me into a frog? Not before I cause Kala more pain than she's ever felt in her life. I don't even need a wand for that." To prove it, Vivian threw the one she was holding across the room. "I've been doing this a lot longer than you. I've evolved."

"If you're so powerful, why do you need Penelope?" I asked, trying to pull my arm out of her grasp.

Her fingers dug into my skin, making me wince. "Because it belongs to *me*. Now, go and find it before I kill the whole lot of you and believe me, it's all I've been dreaming about for the last three months."

"I'm not leaving my sister," said Kendra stubbornly.

"Fine. Stay. But someone better get me my wand," said Vivian, staring at her venomously.

Kendra turned to Willow and Megan. "Find Adrianne. Let her know what's happening."

Looking unsure and frightened, they both nodded and then disappeared.

"Okay, they've left. I'm sure Adrianne will bring you the wand. Now, let her go," said Kendra, still pointing her wand at Vivian.

"Sure," she replied. "Hand over the wand you're holding and I will."

"Don't do it," I told Kendra. "You'll be totally defenseless."

"She already is," said Vivian. "Mark, why don't you take Kala into the bedroom and don't let her out of your sight. I think these two should be separated."

Mark, who'd been silent the entire time, walked over to me. "Come on."

Vivian released my arm.

"I'm not going anywhere without Kendra," I said firmly.

He rolled his eyes, grabbed my arm, and began pulling me across the room.

Furious, I kicked him in the shin as hard as I could. He roared in pain and released me.

"Oh, for Heaven's sake," said Vivian. "Can't you do anything right?" She raised her hand and I was suddenly airborne and flying backward across the room. I slammed into the wall and cried out in pain.

"Kala!" gasped Kendra. She turned her wand on Vivian and cried out, "Depart!"

Vivian disappeared but returned in a matter of seconds. She raised her hand toward Kendra and said, "Enslave." I watched in horror as a rope appeared out of nowhere and wrapped tightly around my sister.

"Liquify rope," said Kendra quickly.

The rope lost its solidity, freeing her.

"Good one," said Vivian, nodding with a smirk. "But not that good." She pointed her finger toward Kendra. "Tongue-tie."

Kendra's eyes widened. She opened her mouth and tried to speak, but it came out in gurgles.

I rushed over to her side and saw in horror that Kendra's tongue appeared to be painfully twisted.

"What's wrong?" laughed Vivian. "At a loss for words? Cat got your tongue?"

Kendra reached into her mouth and tried fixing it with her fingers.

"Don't you ever think that you can get the better of me," said Vivian, her smile fading. "Now, enough foolishness. Mark, get over there and make Kala get into that bedroom before I decide that you're more trouble than you're worth."

His eye twitched but he didn't say anything. Instead, Mark walked toward me, this time with a very determined look on his face.

"If you think I'm going anywhere with you," I said, grabbing Kendra's wand. "You're sadly mistaken."

"Oooo," protested Kendra, a look of alarm on her face.

I grabbed her hand and chanted the words that would bring us to Vail.

CHAPTER TWENTY-TWO

Kala

"Kendra! Kala!" cried Opal, staring up at us in shock. She was alone in Rebecca's living room, her eyes red-rimmed from crying. "How did you get away from Vivian?"

"If she was as smart as she was vain, we'd never have had the chance," I said. "But Vivian obviously thought I couldn't use a White magic wand."

Opal looked at the one I was holding. "It must not be persnickety, like some of them are. Willow!" she hollered.

Willow walked out of the kitchen and when she noticed us, her face lit up. "You got away?!"

"Yes," I said, setting the wand down. "Where's everyone else?"

"Looking for you," said Opal. "Megan went with them."

Kendra and I looked at each other. She tried saying something but her tongue was still messed up.

"Oh crap. We need help," I said. "Vivian chanted a spell that made her tongue, literally, *tied*."

"Willow reached into her pocket and pulled out Juniper. "What was the name of the spell?"

"Tongue-tie," I replied.

Willow cleared her throat. "Juniper, undo the tongue-tie spell."

"I don't think that will work on just any old wand," said Opal. "Unless Vivian used Penelope? I'm pretty sure Clarice still has that wand in her purse."

The spell broke.

Kendra gasped out loud and began talking. "Thank God," she said and touched her tongue.

"Wow. I didn't know it worked on other wand's spells," said Opal, staring at Juniper in amazement.

"Actually, she didn't use a wand," I said. "She didn't need to."

"So she's even more powerful than I thought," said Opal, her eyes haunted. "Thank goodness she didn't get her hands on the three bonding wands. Nothing would have stopped her."

"She told us that she evolved," said Kendra. "Whatever that means."

Just then, Adrianne, Rebecca, Clarice, Adele, and Megan appeared.

"Oh, thank goodness you're both okay," cried Adrianne, rushing toward us. She pulled us both against her and held on tightly. "I have been so worried about you."

"We got away," I said, relieved that nobody had been hurt.

"Did you see Vivian?" asked Kendra.

"No. When we made it to the cabin, she'd already disappeared," she answered, releasing us.

"What about the other witches? And Mark?" I asked.

"They were all gone," said Clarice. "I'm sure that seeing Semora and her coven by our side scared them all away."

"They were with you?" I asked.

"Yes. Semora is livid that Vivian got out and is on the loose," said Clarice. "They're still searching for them."

"What about Bella and Beldora?" asked Kendra. "I can't believe that one of them snuck into the school like that. Pretending to be a teen."

"Pretending to be our friend," said Megan. "I knew there was a reason I didn't like her."

"And I knew there was a reason why she looked familiar," added Willow. "I couldn't see it then but I see it now."

"I wonder how they found out we'd enrolled at the school anyway," said Willow, biting her lower lip.

"They must have heard us talking about it when they were snooping around our house," said Adrianne. "Anyway, don't worry about those two. Semora will take care of them, along with Vivian."

"How did you know we'd gotten away from her?" I asked.

"We weren't sure but decided to stop back here, just in case," said Clarice.

"We're beginning to see just how crafty you girls are," said Adrianne, staring at us proudly.

"How did you get away?" asked Megan.

"Vivian placed a spell on Kendra. I grabbed Kendra's wand and used it to get away," I said. "Apparently I'm able to draw either Black or White magic."

Adrianne smiled. "And Vivian didn't realize that."

"I don't think anyone knew," said Kendra.

"I knew," said Adrianne, putting a hand on my shoulder. She squeezed. "You're capable of Black magic, because of the ties to Vivian. But, you are *meant* for White, because you're a good, kind-hearted person."

"I try to be but there are times..." I said, smirking. "It's not easy."

"Life is not easy but... I'm so proud of you. Of both of you," said Adrianne, touching Kendra's cheek lovingly. "You have no idea."

"We all are," said Clarice. "You have not only stood up to Vivian a number of times, but you've outwitted her."

"Yes, and that's quite an accomplishment, especially for being so young and inexperienced," added Rebecca. "You girls did very well."

"Even so, Vivian is still free," I reminded them.

"Not for long," said Clarice. "Everyone is on the hunt for her and not just Semora's coven. Adele's and Meredith's, too. They'll get her. Don't you worry."

I relaxed. "I hope so."

"Um, I hate to change the subject, but where's Tyler?" asked Kendra.

"Yikes. He's with Bailey and Trixie back at Secrets and they're waiting to hear from us," said Rebecca, taking out her phone. "I'll call and let them know you're okay."

I sat down on the sofa and let out a ragged breath. "Why don't I feel okay?"

"Because we're exhausted and so much has happened," said Kendra, sitting down next to me.

"Yeah. I suppose. Speaking of which, who has my wand?" I asked.

Clarice looked at Adrianne.

"Yes. It's fine. She can have it," said Adrianne.

Clarice opened up her satchel and pulled out both mine and Kendra's towel-wrapped wands. She handed them back to each of us.

"I still think we should destroy the dark wand. If Vivian gets ahold of it, we're going to regret keeping it," said Clarice, watching me unwrap it.

"You are not destroying my wand," I said firmly. "I mean, haven't I proven that I'm responsible enough to keep it?"

"Yes. You have. And don't worry, I've decided to let you keep it," said Adrianne.

"Thank you," I replied, grinning.

She stared at me hard. "But, you'll have to agree to some terms."

"What terms?" I asked, my smile faltering.

"I want you to return to the school," she replied.

"The Roix?" I asked, surprised.

"Yes."

I was about to protest but then remembered the experience that I'd had with the enchanted Fae stones. As much as I wanted to dislike the school, I didn't. I'd even enjoyed the other classes and the thought of returning, wasn't all that bad.

"Willow will be going there, too," said Opal. "We've been talking about it. She really enjoyed herself today."

"Yes. It was amazing," said Willow, her eyes lighting up. "In fact, the thought of being a teacher was something I've always dreamed of doing, but never thought possible. They have a program which would allow me to do that someday. Even better, I could teach magic."

"That's wonderful," said Opal, her eyes filling with proud tears. "I think you'd make a wonderful teacher. You've already helped me with so much since I've been home." She laughed. "I can almost take care of myself now. Almost."

Willow's smile faltered. "I... I don't want to leave you, mom." She sighed. "I'm being selfish."

"No. Don't say that," said Opal, grabbing her daughter's hand. "You have no selfish bones in your body. And listen to me," her voice became stern, "you're going to that school and that's final."

Willow frowned. "But–"

"But nothing. No arguing with your mother, young lady," said Opal, standing her ground.

"She's right. You should go. Besides, you'd see your mother every day afterward," said Clarice, a twinkle in her eye. "You don't have to live there."

Willow's eyes widened in shock. "I don't?"

"No. Not at all. We were going to have you girls stay there only because of Bella and Beldora. I guess we know how badly that played out," said Adrianne dryly.

"What about Kendra?" I asked. "Is she required to go to the school, too?"

Adrianne looked at my sister. "Actually, I really do think it's a good idea for you to go as well, Kendra. Both of you will learn so much."

"As long as we can return home every day and I can still work at Rebecca's part time," said Kendra. "I'm fine with it. You know how I feel about the school in Bayport. I've always felt a little out of place anyway."

"Kendra, of course you can still work for me. In fact, I insist that you do. Things have been running so well with you helping out, I've even managed to go on a date," said Rebecca, pulling out her wand.

"Yes. How did that go, by the way?" asked Kendra. "We never found out."

"It went better than I thought, actually," said Rebecca, staring off into space with a smile.

"If I were you, I'd hit him up on some meat discounts. He owns a butcher shop, right?" asked Clarice.

Rebecca laughed. "Oh, Clarice. Yes, but... I couldn't do that."

"I've been meaning to make that famous chili of mine and meat isn't cheap. Maybe he'll cut me a deal if I mention your name the next time I visit?" said Clarice.

"Don't you dare," said Rebecca, chuckling.

"I'm just teasing. Are you going to go out with him again?" asked Clarice.

"I don't think so. It was nice but we're more friends than anything," she replied. "And when he kissed me goodnight, it felt all wrong. Even he noticed."

"Really? I wonder if he'd be interested in an older woman," said Clarice, now talking more to herself. "How wonderful it would be to have access to a butcher shop."

Adrianne smiled and shook her head.

"Be my guest and ask him out," said Rebecca, smiling in amusement. Her cell phone went off and she looked at an incoming text. "Oh... I have to get going. I'll be right back. Tyler and Bailey would like a lift back here."

"Bailey's coming back here, too?" I asked, feeling a warm rush of pleasure.

"Yes," said Rebecca. "He insists on seeing you. He was worried too, you know."

"Oh." I grinned and looked down.

"I'll be right back," said Rebecca, disappearing.

"I think someone's in love with you," said Megan, nudging me.

"No. We barely know each other," I replied, although I caught myself smiling.

"Speaking of guys and schools, I'm not going back to The Roix, mother. So don't even bother trying to talk me into it," said Megan, turning to look at Adele.

"I figured as much," she replied. "And I'm too tired to argue about it right now."

"Good. Can we go home now?" asked Megan, yawning. "I'm exhausted, too."

"What do you think?" asked Adele, looking toward Adrianne. "Is it safe to go back?"

"I doubt Vivian will be visiting Bayport anytime soon. We have all three bonding wands in our possession and she must know there's a search party looking for her," she replied.

"Yeah and if she does return there," said Megan, turning toward me. "Kala and Kendra are who she'll be seeking. You and I are just small fries, Mom. Probably not even worth her time."

"Don't ever assume that you're not worth anything to Vivian," said Adrianne. "Her enemies are very valuable to her and she's a very rich woman in that respect."

We all knew that was true.

CHAPTER TWENTY-THREE

Kala

When Rebecca returned with Bailey and Tyler, I'd barely gotten out my greeting when I found myself spinning around in his arms.

"Thank God you're okay," he said, setting me back down. "I heard Vivian had you again and almost went insane."

I smiled. "You did, huh?"

His eyes twinkled. "Yes. I should have known you girls could take care of yourselves, though."

"Kala actually saved us and all on her own," said Kendra. "Vivian took her wand away and luckily, Kala was able to use mine. She got us out of there in the nick of time."

"That's my girl," he said, pulling me against him again. He squeezed me so hard I could barely breathe.

"Bailey," I wheezed.

"Oh sorry," he whispered, releasing me. "I'm just so happy you're alive and well."

"Me, too," I said, looking around. Clarice, Rebecca, and Adrianne all seemed to be watching us with interest. Rebecca and I looked at each other and she gave me a knowing smile.

"Uh, would you two like some coffee?" she asked, turning toward Adrianne and Clarice.

"Yes," said Adrianne, catching on. "Sounds lovely."

"I'd like a spot of tea if you have any? Otherwise, I'm sure I have something in my purse," said Clarice, as they disappeared into the kitchen.

Bailey chuckled and looked down. Noticing that I was holding my wand, he frowned. "So, you're still not giving Penelope up?"

"No," I replied.

His blue eyes searched mine. "Are you sure that's the right thing to do?"

"I'm not sure about anything anymore," I admitted. "Other than that none of us can run away from our destiny."

"And you think that Penelope is *your* destiny?" he asked, looking worried.

"I believe that possessing her is my destiny."

"As long as you're the one doing the possessing," he said. "And not vice-versa."

"You really think I'm too weak for the wand, don't you?"

He stared into my eyes again and then sighed. "I know that you're not. I'm actually the one feeling weak right now."

I gave him a questioning look.

He put his hands on my shoulders. "I'm terrified of what owning the wand means which, in essence, is that your life is always going to be in danger. If it's not Vivian wanting to take it from you, it's going to be some other black-hearted soul who'll do anything to obtain it. Your life is always going to be in jeopardy."

"Bailey, my life *is* and always *will be* in jeopardy, regardless. Take for example – Vivian. She spent half of her life searching for us, just to cause harm. It had nothing to do with Penelope. If anything," I nodded toward my wand, "I've never been as protected as I am right now."

He sighed.

I raised the wand. "I'm going to learn how to use this wisely. I swear. In fact, I'm going back to The Roix."

He stared at me in surprise. "You are?"

"Yes. So, you can stop worrying."

"As much as I'm happy to hear that you're returning there, I'm not a big fan of their rules," he said, winking at me.

"You mean about no 'male' visitors?"

He nodded.

"Nothing to concern yourself with. I'm not going to live on campus. You can visit me at night. After school."

His eyebrow rose. "Really? Well, I guess that I can live with that."

"Are you sure?" I teased.

"I'll do what I have to."

"You don't *have* to do anything."

He ran his finger across my cheek. "When it comes to you, I *would* do anything," he said softly.

I blushed.

His eyes traveled around my face and he frowned. "So, are you going back to the school as yourself or this persona?"

"Myself."

"Good, because, no offense, you're pretty right now, even with this disguise, but I miss your true form. When does this potion wear off, anyway?"

I thought back to when we took it. "Within twenty-four hours, so not until around three in the morning."

"Then let's join them for coffee," he said, nodding toward the kitchen.

"Why?"

He gave me a serious look. "Because I'm not leaving here until I get a kiss from the *real* you."

I stood on my tippy-toes and pulled his face to mine. Then I kissed Bailey deeply, surprising him.

"Is that real enough for you?" I whispered when our lips separated.

He gave me a wicked grin. "Let's try it again. Make sure I'm not dreaming," he said, this time pulling me into his arms.

Sighing in pleasure, I dropped the wand as my other, more dashing destiny, claimed my lips and took my breath away.

CHAPTER TWENTY-FOUR

Kala

Within the next two weeks, Kendra and I returned to The Roix, this time enrolling as ourselves. We also kept our wands close at hand at all times. None of the other students recognized that they were special, or bonding wands, but a few of the teachers knew and agreed to keep it a secret.

During this time, the hunt for Vivian, Mark, Beldora, and Bella continued without much luck, but everyone knew it wouldn't be long before they were caught. Especially now that Semora had placed a sizeable bounty on their heads. Now there were witches, vampires, shape-shifters, and a slew of other immortals searching for the group, all of them wanting to collect on a million-dollar reward.

"I didn't know that Semora had that kind of money," I said to Adrianne, after she'd informed me.

"It's not just hers. There are quite a few people that want them, especially Vivian. Even The Roix donated to the cause," she said. "Anyway, enough about them. How was school today? Did you learn some more useful spells?"

Last week I'd learned how to clean my room without lifting a finger, which by far was now one of my favorites. "I learned how to bring a flower back to health," I said.

"By watering it?" she asked, smiling.

I grinned. "That's another way, but you know what I mean."

"Yes, I do. A touch of magic?"

"Yes. A touch of magic. It does wonders, especially when you don't have a green thumb."

She smiled.

I watched as she sprayed wood polish on the coffee table and began to clean it. "Speaking of a touch of magic, why don't you use some for that? You could do the entire living room at once and save a ton of time."

"Sometimes the natural way is still the better way. Like, cleaning your room, for example…"

"How can that be better if I'm spending an hour doing that the old fashioned way versus ten seconds of witchcraft?"

"Because…you can take more pride in your work when you know that you didn't cheat," she said, looking up at me.

"Or, I could be using that time to do something else constructive, like reading or taking a walk," I said. "Or helping you with dinner."

"When was the last time you sat down and read a book that wasn't related to school?" she asked with a sly smile. "Or helped me in the kitchen?"

"I cleaned it yesterday," I said. "After you asked me to."

"With a spell."

I grinned. "Okay but it sure didn't feel like cheating to me. It felt pretty good, actually. I'm definitely not feeling guilty about saving time and making the kitchen sparkle."

She laughed. "I know. Look, I want you to learn what you can about magic, but I don't want you to become dependent on it for everything. If you do, you'll miss out on taking pride in the things you do with your own two hands. You know?"

I sighed. "Yeah. I get it."

"Good. Now, go into the kitchen and start dinner, 'the old fashioned' way," she said, winking at me.

"You know I hate cooking," I told her.

"Even if it's for Bailey?" she asked smirking.

"He's back in town?" I asked, excited. He'd been in California the past few days, helping a friend build a deck for their beach house.

She nodded. "Yes. I ran into him at Secrets earlier today," she said. "He told me where he'd been. I had no idea Bailey did construction on the side."

I nodded. "Not just on the side. He's a carpenter. He really enjoys building things with his hands and someday wants to start his own business."

"Doing what?"

"Making furniture," I replied. "He's shown me pictures of some of his creations. He even made a coffee table out of black walnut for Trixie that was beautiful."

"Oh, wow. Have you ever been to his home?"

"No," I replied. "I know he lives with Trixie, but he's been talking about getting a place of his own."

"Bailey is twenty, isn't he?" she asked, polishing the end table.

"Actually, he looks twenty but I think he's much older," I replied, remembering a conversation we'd had.

She arched her eyebrow. "How old?"

I shrugged. "I don't know. He's not like us. His kind live a lot longer. Why so many questions?"

"I'm just curious. I've never known a shape-shifter before."

Admittedly, it was a strange thought, to be dating someone who could turn into almost anything he wanted. The truth was, I'd mentally blocked that out about him.

"Is it serious between you?" she asked, staring at me.

"No, Mom. We're just dating," I said, feeling uncomfortable. I didn't like being drilled and I didn't know where our relationship would take us.

"Do you love him?"

I stared at her in surprise.

"Do you?"

"Honestly, I don't know." I shrugged. "Maybe."

I definitely had feelings for him but I was also a little frightened. We were so very different.

She smiled. "I'm sorry to be asking you so many questions. It's just... I can tell that he really cares about you, and I'm just..."

"Being you," I said, smiling back at her. "I know."

She walked over and put a hand on my shoulder. "You're young. It doesn't matter whether you know you love someone or are not sure yet. Just have fun with Bailey, but don't jump into something you're not ready for."

"Like what?" I asked.

She shrugged. "I don't know. A commitment."

"You mean like marriage?"

"Maybe."

"I'm definitely not looking for that," I said, chuckling. "So, relax."

Which was the truth. The thought of marrying someone made me anxious. Plus, technically, I was still in high school.

"Okay. I just wanted to find out what was going on with the two of you."

"The one you should be asking these questions to is Kendra," I said.

Just then, my sister stepped into the room. She had her winter jacket on. "What about Kendra?"

"When are you and Tyler getting married?" I teased.

Her face turned pink. "I don't know. He hasn't asked me."

"He'd better not ask you," said Adrianne, smirking.

"Why?" she asked.

Mom's face became serious. "You're too young, that's why."

"I'm eighteen," she said. "An adult."

"That's still too young to get married," said Adrianne. "And I don't care that he's my best friend's son. I'm sure Rebecca would say the same thing."

"Don't worry about me and Tyler," said Kendra, heading toward the front door.

"Where are you off to?" asked Adrianne.

She looked over her shoulder and gave her a cocky grin. "I'm going to meet Tyler so we can get our marriage license. Then we're eloping. See you in a couple days."

Adrianne grabbed a pillow from the sofa and threw it at her.

Kendra laughed and ducked out of the house.

"Mom, just like she said – you really don't need to worry about Kendra or me," I said, walking toward the kitchen. "Neither of us are in a rush to tie the knot. And if we were, you'd be the first to know. Well, maybe the third to know."

She gave me a wry smile. "Are you really just eighteen?"

I smiled. "After the last few months, I've been feeling a lot older. So, what should I make for dinner?"

"There's some chicken in the refrigerator. Surprise us. Just, don't use magic."

"Don't use magic? Fine. It's your stomach," I said, winking.

CHAPTER TWENTY-FIVE

Kala

When Bailey arrived, he was dressed in a black slacks and a pale blue sweater that brought out his eyes.

"Are those for me?" I asked, nodding toward the dark pink roses he held.

"Actually, they're for your mother," he said, with a lopsided grin. "Sorry."

I shrugged and smiled. "It's okay."

He leaned over and kissed me on the lips quickly. "I have something else for you."

My eyes widened. "Oh. Okay. You didn't have to bring anything, you know."

"I know," he said and then smiled down at my outfit. I hadn't really known what to wear but settled on an off-white cashmere sweater and a simple black skirt. My hair was up in a loose bun and I wore a pair of hoop earrings that he'd complimented me on before. "You look and smell beautiful, by the way."

I blushed. "Thanks."

"Bailey. Welcome," said Adrianne, walking into the living room.

"Thank you. Here," he said, holding out the flowers.

Her eyes widened. "For me?"

"Yes. I remembered that you once mentioned loving dark pink roses and saw them on my way here."

"That's very kind of you," she said, smelling them. "I'll go and put them in water."

He nodded.

Adrianne turned around and walked out of the room.

"Dinner is almost ready," I said.

"It smells great."

"Thanks. I made it myself," I said. "I just hope it tastes half as good as it smells."

"I have a feeling it's going to be my new favorite meal."

I wasn't so sure but decided not to mention my horrible cooking abilities. "So, how was your trip?"

"Good. You want to see a picture of the deck we built?" he asked, looking excited.

He reminded me of a little boy, showing off one of his toys. I smiled. "Sure."

Bailey pulled out his cell phone and showed me a bunch of pictures.

"Wow. You helped build that?' I asked, impressed. "It's nice. Huge."

"I'm going back next week to help them put in a hot tub and gazebo."

My face fell. He'd just gotten back. "How long are you going to be gone?"

His smile fell. "Actually, I'm going to be away for a few weeks. It's why I wanted to see you tonight."

"What do you mean? Where are you going?"

"I'm going to Europe for a family reunion. Trixie will be joining me, of course."

I stared at him in surprise. "Oh. I didn't know you had family in Europe."

"There are a lot of things you don't know about me," he said, walking to the sofa. He sat down and patted the seat next to him.

I walked over and sat down next to him. "True. Why don't you tell me a little more about yourself then? I mean, if you want to. You don't have to."

He chuckled. "No. I do want to. You obviously know I'm a shape-shifter."

I nodded."

"How do you feel about that?"

I shrugged. "I don't know. How do you feel about me being a witch?"

He laughed. "Other than knowing that I'd better not make you mad, I'm fine with it. Actually, more than fine. I think it's pretty cool, actually."

I smiled. "I'm beginning to feel the same way."

"And then there's me." He took my hand and squeezed it. "Obviously, my DNA is quite different than yours."

"You look..." I didn't know how to say it without offending him. "Uh, like an average guy. I mean, much better than average."

He grinned. "Thanks."

"Is this your real form?"

"Yes, it is."

Phew. That was a relief. "How many other forms can you take?"

"There are an infinite amount of forms I can shape into," he said. "However, the bigger they are, the more energy it takes."

I nodded. "So... do you feel things like a mortal man?"

"I am a mortal man, only with a very special gift. I live. I die. I feel. The only difference is that my cells allow me to change into whatever I set my mind to. For a limited amount of time."

I studied his face. "Do you age the same as us?"

"How old do you think I am?"

"You look like you're about twenty. Twenty-one maybe?"

"I am twenty-one."

"Really?" I smiled. I was almost worried that he was going to tell me he was fifty. That would have been a little weird. "How long is your lifespan?"

"Same as yours."

I nodded. "Okay."

We sat there in silence for a few seconds.

"What about children?" I asked.

He gave me a small smile. "What about them?"

"Can you have them?"

"No."

"Oh."

He laughed. "Men can't get pregnant. I guess they don't teach that at magic school?"

I hit him in the arm playfully. "You know what I meant."

"I do. I'm sorry," said Bailey, still chuckling. "Yes. We can father children or have them, depending on our gender."

"Will your kids also be shape-shifters?"

"Depends on the mother. If she's a shape-shifter, definitely. If she's not, there's a fifty-fifty chance that the child will have the same gift."

"That makes sense."

He grabbed my hand and slid his fingers through mine. "I have something for you," he said, reaching into the pocket of his trousers. He pulled out a small giftwrapped box and handed it to me.

"What is this?" I asked, feeling a rush of pleasure.

"Open it and find out."

I unwrapped the box and opened it. Inside was a beautiful pendant necklace made of sapphire and gold.

"It's beautiful," I said, taking it out of the box.

"I'm glad you like it. I had it made for you."

I smiled and slipped it over my head. It was a longer chain, so it rested near my heart. "You did?"

"Yes. I picked out the sapphires, because it matches your eyes."

My smile widened. "I can't believe you actually had this made for me. It's gorgeous."

"I wanted you to be protected. When I'm gone," he said.

I stared at him in confusion. "I don't understand. What does that mean?"

"It's enchanted. It will make you invisible if needed. All you have to do is hold it in your fist and and say my name."

"Are you serious?" I asked, laughing.

He nodded.

"Should I try it right now?"

"Go ahead."

I wrapped my hand around the pendant and said, "Bailey." As I stared down at my fist, it disappeared, along with my arm and every other part of my body.

"Oh, my God, this is incredible!" I said loudly.

My mother took that moment to walk into the living room. She looked around. "Where's Kala?"

"I'm right here," I said.

Adrianne blinked in confusion.

I let go of the pendent and materialized. "Ta-da!"

She smiled and looked down at my necklace. "Wow. Where did you get that?"

"I got it for her," said Bailey, looking pleased with himself. "For added protection. In case she ever needs it."

"Those are expensive," she said, staring at him in disbelief.

"What's money compared to a life?" he said, looking at me. "Especially one that's more precious than the stone around her neck."

Mom looked at me and smiled.

My heart fluttered. "That's so sweet."

He grabbed my hand and kissed my knuckles. "Now I can worry less about you when I'm in Norway."

"Why are you going to Norway, Bailey?" asked Adrianne.

He began explaining to her about his family reunion. I sat back and listened. When or eyes met and he smiled at me again, it was then I realized that I had fallen in love with Bailey without realizing it. It wasn't because of how gorgeous he was or the fact that he had special powers. It wasn't even for the necklace. I loved him because of the way he made me feel every time we were together and the fact that every time he looked at me, I could see he felt the same way. The realization brought a goofy grin to my face.

"What's so funny?" asked my mother, noticing.

"Nothing," I said, wiping the smile off of my face. "So, when's dinner going to be ready?"

"I don't know. You're the one who put it in the oven. You tell me," said Adrianne.

Before I could answer, the fire alarm went off in the kitchen.

I shot up off of the sofa. "Oh crap! Is that coming from the kitchen?"

Adrianne groaned and rushed out of the living room.

I looked at Bailey. "About my cooking... I should probably tell you...."

"Kala!" hollered my mother angrily.

He grinned. "Actually, we'll have that conversation later. Now might be a good time for you to disappear."

I smiled.

CHAPTER TWENTY-SIX

Kala

The chicken dinner was indeed ruined, so we ordered a pizza. When we were finished, Bailey and I watched a movie and then, after a long kiss goodbye, he took off.

As I was getting ready for bed, Vee began speaking to me again. It had been awhile and I'd thought it had gone away for good. Apparently, I was wrong.

Bailey wants to control you...

Frowning, I tried ignoring Vee.

I know you think you love him, but he's not worthy of it.

I sucked in my breath. "Penelope?"

Silence.

I took out my wand. "Are you the one, somehow, talking to me in my head?"

"Of course not," said the wand.

"Are you sure?"

"I don't lie. Why should I?"

I didn't know if wands could lie or not. It made me uneasy.

Just then, Kendra walked into the bedroom.

"Wow. That's beautiful," Kendra said, noticing my new necklace as she crossed the room.

I covered my hand over it. "I know. But here's what's even more beautiful," I said, and then whispered. "Bailey."

"Oh, yeah, what's that?"

I disappeared.

She turned around and gasped. "Kala!?"

"I'm here."

"How in the world did you disappear into thin air?"

"The necklace is enchanted," I told her, reappearing.

"It is? I want one!" she pouted.

"This was a gift," I said, smiling down at it proudly. "From Bailey."

"He must really like you," she said, smiling.

"That's what I'm thinking," I said.

She gave me a knowing look. "Actually, with a gift like that, he most certainly loves you."

"I hope so."

Her eyes widened. "You *hope* so? So you love him, too?"

"Yes."

She squealed. "I knew it!"

"He's going away for a few weeks. To Europe. I'm going to miss the heck out of him."

"You don't have to. You're a witch. I'm sure you can find a way to see him," she said, grinning. "If you want to."

"I know. We'll see. I don't want to be, like, some kind of stalker."

"You're his girlfriend. You're allowed to be a little bit stalkerish. Especially if you're a witch."

I laughed. "Maybe."

"Oh, by the way… I heard that Megan is going to be returning to The Roix. She broke up with her boyfriend and wants to seclude herself from all men in general for a while."

"Oh. Okay. I hope that doesn't mean she's going to be even more moodier than she was before."

"You know her. She's going to be a nightmare." Kendra yawned. "I'm exhausted. By the way, I heard we're each going to be using the enchanted stones in class again. In fact, we each get to visit with a fairy for a couple of minutes."

That perked me right up. "Really? How fascinating. I can't wait."

"I know, right?"

"Kendra?"

"What?"

"I know this sounds like a weird question, but… does your wand talk to you in your head?"

She gave me a surprised look. "What?"

"I keep hearing this voice in my head." I bit my lower lip. "It tells me things."

"Chloe doesn't. We hardly talk but if she has something she wants to say, she speaks it loud and clear."

"Hmm… Do you think that wands can lie?"

"I have no idea. Maybe you should ask one of the teachers tomorrow."

"Maybe I should."

"Or ask Mom."

"No. She'll get anxious about it and tell me to get rid of Penelope," I said.

She sighed. "Yeah. You're probably right. Just ask one of the teachers. They'll know for sure."

Don't trust anyone... whispered Vee. *Just me.*

I frowned.

"What's wrong?" asked Kala.

"Nothing," I said, looking away. I wasn't sure if I was freaking myself out, if it was my subconscious talking, or something else entirely. I certainly didn't want my sister thinking I was crazy. "Nothing. I'm going to bed. Goodnight."

"Goodnight."

CHAPTER TWENTY-SEVEN

Kala

The next morning, I wore my necklace to school, hiding the pendant under my robe. As Kendra and I made our way to our Enchanted Objects class, we bumped into Megan.

"Hey, how's it going?" I asked. She was back to her real self, only this time, her hair was colored neon pink and it was in a bob.

She nodded toward the ceiling. "It was going fine until one of those poltergeists started following me. It's like I have a note on my forehead that says 'Haunt me'."

"Have you been ignoring them?" I asked.

"I tried but it got to be too much, so I told one of them where to go…" she mumbled. "Talk about a mistake."

One of the poltergeists flew next to Megan and blew in her ear.

"See what I mean? They won't leave me alone!" she growled, trying to wave it away.

"Throw salt at them," said a girl walking by.

"Salt?" repeated Megan.

The other student raised her thumb.

"Hmm… can't hurt," said Megan as another spirit stopped in front of her face and screeched loudly.

"Which class are you headed off to?" I asked, ignoring the ghost.

"Enchanted Objects," she said, glaring at the entity.

"So are we. Let's go together," I replied.

She followed us to class and we sat together in the back again.

"Good morning," said Ms. Benky, closing the door behind her. "I bet you're all excited about today."

"What's going on?" whispered Megan.

"Enchanted stones again," whispered Kendra.

"Sweet," replied Megan, actually smiling.

"First of all, we have another new student. Megan Fisher. She's also from Bayport," said Ms.Benky. "Why don't you stand up?"

Sighing, Megan stood up.

One of the poltergeists pulled at her robe, making it billow out. It then made a loud flatulence noise. Megan let out an angry growl.

"Ignore them," said Ms. Benky, trying not to laugh.

"It doesn't seem to work for me," said Megan, frustrated. "And now... they just won't leave me alone."

The teacher opened up her desk and pulled out a salt shaker. She walked over and handed it to Megan. "The next time one of them bothers you, throw salt at it. They hate the stuff."

"Thank you," said Megan, sighing in relief.

Ms. Benky went back to her desk and took out the enchanted Fae stones. "Today, each of you are going back to Fae Valley. This time, you'll be invited to interview one of the fairies."

Everyone began talking at once.

"You are allowed three questions," said the teacher, raising her voice over ours. "No more."

"Do we get to pick the fairy?" asked one of the other students.

"No. You'll get one who has volunteered and in no particular order. Now, this is a very special gift they're giving to us. It's important that the questions you ask are both appropriate and sensitive. Don't be rude."

One girl raised her hand. "Can we ask them about their families?"

"Yes. Of course," she replied. "Just use common sense and please, don't ask anything that might offend them. Understand? I don't think I can stress that enough."

Everyone nodded in agreement.

"Okay. So, who would like to go first?" she asked.

Everyone raised their hands.

This time, Ms. Benky selected Emily.

"Oh, my God, this is so awesome," she said, rushing to the front of the class.

Fortunately, I was able to take my turn soon after hers. This time, when I entered into the other realm, I walked under the tree's leaves and found the same blonde fairy I'd met during my last visit.

"Hi," I said, staring at her in surprise. Instead of flying, she was seated under the tree and the size of a full-grown adult human.

"Hi," she answered, smiling warmly. "My name is Shehah."

"I'm Kala," I replied.

"I know. Please," she said, waving toward the grass next to her. "Sit."

"What happened to your wings?" I asked, noticing they were gone.

"They're tucked in behind me. That's one question. We are only allowed to answer three. So, please, choose them wisely," she said.

"Okay," I said, sitting down across from her. "I have so many things that I want to ask. I wish..."

"I know. I have many things I would like to ask as well," she said in a soft voice. "But, at least we have this time together."

I nodded. I could tell by the way she was smiling that she was enjoying herself just as much as me.

"Okay. I guess my first question is... what is the one thing that makes you extremely happy?"

She smiled. "When I know that I've helped make someone else's life... brighter."

"Me too," I said, smiling. "Okay... next question, do you have a mate?"

She nodded. "Yes. His name is Dahlan."

"Let me guess, he's really handsome too, right?" I asked. The females were beautiful. I could only assume the men were good looking, too.

"I'm sorry. I can't answer any more of your questions," she said, giving me a sympathetic look.

Crap. I should have thought out my questions better. "That's okay. I understand. I'm sure he's cute."

With a twinkle in her eye, she looked around and then nodded.

I smiled.

She looked up toward the tree. "Our time is up. They know I've answered your questions. I must go."

"Well, it was nice talking to you. I wish we could meet and have a real conversation," I said, standing up.

"Me too," she replied, also standing.

"If you're allowed to ask me a question, I'd be happy to answer," I said.

"I am not supposed to ask questions but I was never told that," she looked around and lowered her voice, "I couldn't warn you..."

My eyes widened. "Warn me? About what?"

"Your wand. It's going to destroy someone very close to you," she said, her eyes taking on a faraway look. "But, through death you will also find closure."

I stared at her in horror. "What do you mean?"

She glanced up toward the castle. "I can't answer that. You must go."

"But–"

She shrunk back down to her normal size and flew away.

CHAPTER TWENTY-EIGHT

Kala

I wasn't sure what to make of Shehah's warning, but it was definitely troubling.

"What happened?" asked Kendra.

I told her about the conversation that I had with the Fae.

"That was strange. Do you think they can tell the future?"

"I have no idea," I replied.

"It must have something to do with Vivian," replied Kendra.

"But, we're not close," I said.

She sighed. "True."

The rest of the hour was spent, watching the others return from Fae Valley and learning about their conversations.

"So, what have we found out about the Fae?" asked the teacher, holding a piece of chalk.

"That they live to be over one-hundred," said Emily.

"Yes," said Ms. Benky, writing the fact down. "What else?"

"That they have spouses and children, just like we do," said Kendra.

"Good," said the teacher, adding it to the list. "What else?"

"That their diets consist of fruit, nuts, and vegetables," said Emily.

Ms. Benky nodded. "Yes."

"I learned that they have enemies," said Megan.

We all turned to look at her.

"Trolls are their main enemies," she continued. "They can't stand each other."

"Now that, I did know," said Ms. Benky.

"Did anyone ask if they can grant wishes?" asked Emily. "I was going to ask, but forgot."

"I did," said Willow. "But unfortunately, I ran out of questions and couldn't ask 'how' or 'why'."

The teacher chuckled. "That's not something they usually have a straight answer for anyway. Legend has it that if you save their life, they'll grant you a wish. Unfortunately, I've never heard of anyone who's actually done that, so I have no idea if it's actually true or not."

"Maybe that's why they separate themselves from us. So they don't have to grant any wishes," said Emily.

"Oh, I'm quite sure that's not the only reason," said Ms. Benky.

"I learned that the Fae enjoy helping others," I said. "At least the one that I spoke to admitted to it."

"Most of them do, just as we do. We're very different from each other and yet, we basically want the same things ... like love, acceptance, and a happy, fruitful life," said the teacher.

"Some of us needing more 'fruit' than others," I mumbled, thinking of Vivian and her selfish needs.

"Very true," said the teacher, hearing me.

The bell rang and she set her chalk down. "We'll talk more about the Fae tomorrow."

As I was walking out of the classroom with the others, Ms. Benky called me over.

"Yes?" I asked.

"I almost forgot, but Dean Marigold wanted me to have you bring the enchanted Fae stones to her office. She usually locks them up at night in her safe, and I have no other classes today. Do you mind?"

"Not at all, but why me?" I asked.

"She wanted to talk to you about Vivian," said Ms. Benky, lowering her voice. All the teachers in the school now knew of Vivian. Even Sybil, who claimed that she had no idea that Dorie had actually been Beldora or that Bella had used her to get to us. Apparently, she hadn't even known that the two witches were kicked out of their coven.

"Oh. Okay."

"I'm sure I don't have to tell you to be very careful with those stones," she said, lowering her voice. "Whatever you do, *don't* lose them."

"I won't."

She handed me the bag and I stuck them into my pocket.

"Should I wait until lunchtime?"

"No. Go now," said the teacher. "The longer you keep them in your possession, the more worried I become. No offense."

I laughed. "None taken. They're valuable. I get it."

She grinned. "Did you enjoy class today?"

"It was incredible. I do have a question, though."

"What is it?" she asked.

"Can the Fae tell the future?"

Her forehead wrinkled. "Why do you ask?"

I didn't want to get Shehah in trouble, so I kept her warning to myself. "I just heard a rumor that they could."

"Not all of them can. Just a few. It's the same with humans. There are some with real psychic abilities and there are those who claim to know the future and lie about it. For profit, of course."

I nodded. "Yeah, I suppose that makes sense."

Her cell phone went off.

"I'd better take this," she said. "Go and get those rocks to the dean, please."

"Yeah. I'll go now."

I walked out of the class and found Kendra, Willow, and Megan waiting for me.

"What did she want?" asked Kendra.

"I'm supposed to bring the enchanted stones to the dean's office," I said in a low voice.

"That's kind of weird. Why *you*?" asked Megan.

"It sounds like she might have some news about Vivian," I said.

"I'm coming with you," said Kendra. "I'd like to find out if she knows something."

"Okay," I said.

"Let us know what you find out," said Megan. "I can't skip class. Not on my first day."

"Yeah. Hopefully it's good news," said Willow.

I nodded. "We'll soon find out, I guess."

Kendra and I headed to Marigold's office. We knocked on the door and she called me in.

"Oh. Kendra. You're here, too. Even better," said Marigold with a wide smile. "Why don't you both take a seat?"

We sat down across from her.

"So, I heard you wanted to talk about Vivian?" I said. "Do you have some news for us?"

She nodded. "Yes. I do, actually. Did you bring the stones with you?" she asked, standing up.

I pulled the bag out of my pocket and handed it to her.

"Excellent," she said, looking inside with a wide grin.

"So, what's going on?" I asked, leaning back in the chair. "Did they catch her yet?"

"Not yet. Apparently, she's on the loose and somewhere here in Canada," Marigold said with a grave expression.

Alarmed, Kendra and I glanced at each other.

"She wants her wand back," said the dean. "And if she gets it back, you know your life will be in jeopardy."

"As far as we're concerned, our lives have always been in jeopardy," I said dryly.

"I'm sure you're right," said Marigold, unlocking the safe. She set the bag of stones inside and then turned to us. "I think, under the circumstances, we should lock up your wands in my safe. If she gets into this school and obtains them, especially yours, Kala, we're all in trouble."

"And if you ask me, I think we should just go home," said Kendra, looking at me. "Until we know more."

"No. I want to keep my wand. If she finds us, I want protection," I said firmly.

"Let me ask you – Vivian was the previous owner of the dark wand, correct?" asked Marigold.

I nodded.

The dean's face darkened. "Then she will have some kind of influence on the wand, which means, that it won't be able to protect you the way another wand could."

I stared at her in surprise. "You're saying that if I tried using Penelope on her, that nothing would happen?"

"More than likely, she would be immune to the effects," she replied.

I groaned.

"So, you see...your life, along with everyone else's in this school, is at risk *because* you're carrying it on your person. Knowing that, I'm going to have to ask you to hand the wand over," she said.

"That's really not a good idea," I replied, when she held out her hand.

She laughed. "No, how can I be so stupid? Please, put the wand in the safe. I'd almost forgotten that I couldn't touch it."

I looked at my sister, still unsure of what to do.

"It might be a good idea. Just until we know that Vivian has been caught," said Kendra.

I let out a frustrated sigh and stood up. "Fine."

"I know how much the wand means to you," said Marigold as I walked over to the safe. "And I understand how hard it is to part with. But rest assured, you're making a wise choice."

I placed the wand into the safe and looked at Marigold. "Do you have another wand I can use? At least until the end of the day? I still have the other one you gave me back in Bayport."

"I'm sure I can find you something," she replied.

"I'd appreciate it," I said, walking away from the safe.

"Although," the dean laughed, "I don't think you're going to need a wand where you're going, sweetheart."

"Oh, my God," gasped Kendra, shooting up out of her chair.

I turned around and in Marigold's place stood Vivian with a smile that made my blood run cold.

"Did you really think I'd give up so easily?" she asked. "Or that any of those weak, stupid coven witches could actually capture me?"

"What have you done with Marigold?" I asked.

"I think the dean is the least of your worries," said Vivian. She reached into the safe and pulled out Penelope. "Finally. I have my precious wand back."

"It's mine now," I snapped. "Give it back to me!"

"Yours?" she snorted.

"Yes, mine!" I hollered.

Vivian's smile fell and her face contorted in pain. "No…"

Kendra and I looked at each other. Something was happening.

"How can this be?" Vivian gasped, staring down at her hand.

We watched as it began to glow a familiar red color.

"It's not bonding with her," said Kendra, shocked.

"What have you done to my wand?" screeched Vivian, trying to release it. "Penelope?! What's the meaning of this? Speak to me!"

"Do not make demands of me, witch. You are not worthy," retorted the wand in a haughty voice.

Vivian glared down at Penelope. "What do you mean? *I'm* not worthy?!"

"Silence, wicked one! I have bonded with Kala. I prefer her over you."

"But you were made to serve a dark master," cried Vivian, the light moving up her arm toward her shoulder. "You can't tell me Kala fits those credentials!"

Kendra looked at me.

I shrugged my shoulders. As far as I was concerned, Vivian was actually right about something for once.

"You forget that I was made to serve either side, White or Black magic. Her inner strength is much stronger than yours, even as young as she is. You are selfish and serve only yourself. Her willingness to serve others before herself is a much stronger attribute. You are not worthy of a wand like me. She, on the other hand, is."

"So, what you're some kind of self-righteous wand now?" snarled Vivian, sinking to her knees.

"No. I am simply a wand who can choose her master. I have made my choice," said Penelope. "And, it's not you."

"Your fault," whispered Vivian, staring up at us. "I should have never given birth to the two of you. You've made my life hell."

"You were the one who made ours hell," I said. "And now, neither of us have to worry about the other anymore."

She glared at me as the red light flowed into her chest and spread everywhere else. Kendra and I both watched as the woman who'd once given us life and then spent most of her own trying to take it back, lost hers.

CHAPTER TWENTY-NINE

Kala

We sent a message to Adrianne and she arrived with Clarice, Adele, and Semora in less than two minutes.

"Well, good riddance," said Semora, staring down at Vivian's still body. "Hopefully, she'll stay dead this time, too."

Her words were cold but I couldn't help but feel the same way. Even seeing her lying there, I almost didn't trust that she was really gone. Part of me expected her to shoot back up and then laugh in our faces.

"You know what we need to do?" said Kendra.

"What?" I asked.

"We need to get rid of the wands," she said softly, staring down at Chloe. "All three of them."

"No," I said, gripping mine tightly. "There's no reason to. Especially now. Vivian is dead and as long as Willow's wand isn't used to resurrect her, we'll be fine."

"That's the thing," said Kendra, looking into my eyes. "We can't take that chance. Juniper has already saved her twice. Once from death and once from the globe. The wand must be destroyed and... in all fairness, yours need to be disposed of, too."

"I agree," said Willow, walking into Marigold's office with Ms. Benky. "And, so that we don't have to go through something like this again, I'm willing to give my wand up."

"It's not an easy decision, I know. But, it's the right one," said Kendra.

The thought of losing Penelope tore me up inside.

"I don't understand why we can't just get rid of Willow's wand?" I said quickly. "We can find her another wand that's powerful."

"Come on, you know it wouldn't be fair," said Kendra.

I looked at Adrianne and the others, expecting them to side with Kendra, but nobody said anything. Something told me that my mother was leaving it up to me knowing that it would be a choice I'd have to live with.

"Could we take some time to think about it?" I asked. "Just a couple of days?"

"I say we do it now, while the memory of how destructive the wands can be is fresh in our heads," said Kendra.

"I'm not going to change my mind," said Willow. "I would rather dispose of the wands then have to worry about Vivian coming back."

I sighed.

Don't let them destroy me...

The blood rushed to my head. I stared down at my wand. "Penelope?"

"Yes?" said the wand innocently.

I frowned. "Were you just in my head?"

The wand didn't answer.

Adrianne and Clarice looked at each other.

"Answer me," I said firmly.

"Maybe," she replied.

"Maybe? You mean 'yes'. You *lied* to me earlier. It was you all along," I said angrily. She *was* Vee.

"We have bonded. We're as one now," said the wand. "Our minds will always be connected."

"Still, you were dishonest and should have told me," I snapped.

"I'm sorry. I thought I could help you," said the wand.

"Help me? What was it you said before? Oh yeah, you're not a therapist," I replied.

"I only wanted to guide you toward intelligent choices," said Penelope.

"You mean what you considered to be intelligent choices," I argued.

"I was always on your side."

"That's not the point. You were dishonest when I questioned you about hearing voices in my head."

"Yes. I apologize," said Penelope.

She was sorry but did wands really have regrets? Did they have feelings? It seemed that way. If that was the case, however, it also meant that my wand was willing to act on hers and that could be very dangerous.

Adrianne put a hand on my shoulder. "Are you okay?"

I smiled grimly "Apparently, wands can lie."

"Apparently they can," she said. "So, what are you going to do?"

"What I have to, I guess," I replied.

Think about this before you make a rash decision. I can make you a powerful sorceress. More powerful than you could ever imagine. You'd be giving all of that up if you destroy me.

I don't want to be powerful. Not like that, I told Penelope.

I also didn't want anyone knowing what I was thinking. Not even my wand. It made me wonder if Penelope had actually influenced some of my earlier decisions, which was an unsettling thought.

"Kala? Are you okay?" asked Adrianne, staring at me with concern.

"I'm fine. Just feeling a little gullible," I said quietly.

Thankfully, my mother didn't rub in the fact that she'd warned me. She only gave me a reassuring smile and squeezed my shoulder.

"Penelope," I said.

"Yes?" asked the wand.

I took a deep breath and released it. I wasn't sure how she was going to react, but it had to be done. I knew that now. "I want you to know that it's been a pleasure having you serve me. And even though we've hit a glitch, it was still an amazing experience," I said sadly.

I knew I couldn't keep the wand. It was too dangerous. As much as I wanted to believe that I would always be the one in control, I wouldn't truly know for sure. Even if Penelope never actually influenced me, I would always question my decisions. It would drive me insane.

The wand let out a weary sigh of her own. "The pleasure has been mine. Kala, I understand why you're relinquishing me and it only confirms what I already knew. *You* are worthy. In fact, you are worthy, brave, and more honorable than any of the witches I've served in the past."

I smiled. "Thank you, Penelope."

"So, this is really goodbye?" she asked.

"Yes. I'm afraid so," I said, running my thumb along the handle absently.

"Good luck to you in your future endeavors, Kala."

"Thank you."

One last thing, said Penelope. *He really is worthy. You should know that.*

I already do.

With a throaty laugh, the wand sparkled brightly and then became silent.

"Kendra," said Adrianne. She nodded toward Chloe. "Now would probably be a good time to say your goodbyes, if you wish to, that is."

"Oh. Yeah," said Kendra.

I thought I was a sap, but I watched as my sister said a teary goodbye to Chloe.

"Well, that was much harder than I thought," said Kendra, wiping her cheeks afterward.

I could only smile. If anyone would have told me that Kendra or I could grieve over a piece of wood a year ago, I'd have laughed in their face. But, these wands weren't just objects. They'd become extensions of ourselves. I still wasn't sure if that was a good thing, but I definitely knew that it could turn into a bad thing. At least with wands as powerful as ours.

When Willow was finished saying goodbye to Juniper, who was still a wand of little words, we stuck all three of them into a burlap sack.

"What now?" I asked, looking at Adrianne.

"I think we should burn them," she said. "In Salem."

"Very good idea," said Semora. "It's All Hallow's Eve tomorrow, and there will be a full moon. A perfect night to send them off."

"It's fitting," said Adrianne, a wistful look on her face. "And what of Vivian?"

"We'll bury her next to your mother," said Semora. "Lisbeth would have wanted that. She loved you both."

"And she was the one person Vivian actually loved, I think," replied Adrianne.

"We're not contacting the police?" asked Ms. Benky, who'd been standing there watching us quietly the entire time.

"No," said Clarice. "As you know, they're not even allowed in this school and wouldn't have a clue about the bonding wands. Imagine *that* kind of paperwork?"

She had a point.

"Does anyone know what happened to Marigold?" asked Ms. Benky, looking around.

"She's fine," said Clarice. "Bella and Beldora had her tied up in her sleeping quarters. Luckily, two elves helped her escape. Candace and Sherry. She should be here any minute."

"What about Bella and Beldora?" I asked. "Are they still on the loose?"

"Not for long," said Semora. "Without Vivian, they're going to panic, which means they'll make another stupid move, something the two of them are famous for. Don't worry, we'll find them."

"And Mark? What ever happened to him?" asked Kendra.

"That, we're not too sure of. But, he's young and has no one now. I'm sure he'll pop up like a bad penny somewhere though," said Semora, smiling in amusement.

The thought of Mark being free didn't worry me too much. Now that Vivian was gone, I didn't think he was much of a threat.

"Don't worry about that boy," said Clarice. "I heard from a friend that he was spotted trying to leave the country – and this was before Vivian died. I think he might have had enough of her."

"Probably. He was locked away with her for a few weeks," said Adrianne.

"Still, he's gutless," said Semora. "If we find him, we find him. I'm not going to lose any sleep, though, if we don't."

"If you do find him, I want you to bring him to me," said Adrianne. "Please. He is family, after all. Maybe we can reform him?"

"Reform him? I doubt it," said Kendra with a sneer. "Don't you remember what kind of a jerk he was?"

"Even so. Please, Semora?" asked Adrianne.

"If you wish," she said. "We'll hand him over to you if we catch him."

"Thank you," said Adrianne.

Marigold took that moment to arrive with the two elves.

"Is everyone okay?" she exclaimed, looking disheveled.

"We're fine. What about you?" asked Clarice, placing a hand on her back.

"I'm fine. Oh my," she said, staring down at Vivian. "Is she really dead?"

"Yes," I replied.

"What happened?" the dean asked.

"She tried taking her wand back and it wouldn't accept her," said Adrianne.

Marigold sighed. "At least it's over."

Adrianne let out a sigh. "Yes. It is."

"Forgive me," said Marigold, her eyes softening. "I know there was no love lost between you, but I'm still very sorry for your loss."

Adrianne nodded.

"We should take her to Salem," said Semora. "Get her out of here before others notice what's going on."

"Yes. That wouldn't be a very good thing," said Marigold. "The rest of the staff doesn't need to know about this."

Adrianne kneeled down next to Vivian. I watched in shock as she leaned over and kissed her twin tenderly on the cheek. "As much as I disliked you and everything you did to our family, I always, *always* loved you," she whispered.

Kendra and I looked at each other.

Smiling sadly, I walked over and put my arm over my twin's shoulder. "If that doesn't make you appreciate what we have together, I don't know what will."

She leaned her head against mine. "I know. I think their messed up relationship actually brought us closer together though. Pretty warped, huh?"

Kendra was right. In fact, the past few months had made me realize just how precious our family was and the people in our lives. After all, objects are still just... objects. Even the enchanted ones. I'd also learned that obsessing over a possession can sometimes destroy part of a person. Possibly even the part that is capable of love.

"You can say that again," I said, my heart heavy for Adrianne and the pain she'd gone through by loving a sister who couldn't return the favor. Just as she sacrificed so much over the years to keep us safe, I knew our love would always be there for the woman who raised us as her own. As far as I was concerned, *that* was the only kind of magic worth dying for...

Printed in Great Britain
by Amazon